W9-AXV-330

TWO-MINUTE MYSTERIES

BY DONALD J. SOBOL

SCHOLASTIC BOOK SERVICES
NEW YORK • TORONTO • LONDON • AUCKLAND • SYDNEY • TOKYO

For Gloria and Bill Keithan

Other books by the author available from
Scholastic Book Services:

* *More Two-Minute Mysteries*
* *Still More Two-Minute Mysteries*
* *Encyclopedia Brown: Boy Detective*
* *Encyclopedia Brown Finds the Clues*
* *Encyclopedia Brown Gets His Man*
* *Encyclopedia Brown Keeps the Peace*
* *Encyclopedia Brown Strikes Again*

ISBN: 0-590-08111-X

29 28 27 26 25 24 23 22   01/8

Printed in the U.S.A.   06

The Case of the
ANGRY CHEF

Hawkins, the marine, stared in amazement at Inspector Winters.

"I never heard of a restaurant called Pasquale's Pizzeria," he objected. "I wasn't ever in it, I didn't rob it, and I certainly didn't shoot anybody."

"A marine answering your description wounded the owner and cleaned out the cash register," said the inspector. "You didn't know?"

"Am I supposed to?" protested Hawkins. "There must be several thousand marines in this town."

"But only one was running along 42nd Street five minutes after the holdup," snapped the inspector.

"Sure I ran," retorted Hawkins. "Look, I was standing idly in a doorway wondering what to do when this fat guy wearing a white apron and chef's hat comes charging at me. He's waving a butcher knife and he's screaming, 'He shot the boss!' So I ran."

"You were innocent, but you ran?"

"He had that big knife."

"Then what did you do?"

"A cop saw us and grabbed me. It wasn't any use to argue. So I went back to the restaurant with the cop and a couple of customers said I might be the marine who held up the place. They weren't sure."

That night Haledjian read the transcript of the questioning.

"Hawkins is your man," he said. "No mistake about it!"

How did Haledjian know?

Hawkins asserted he'd never heard of the restaurant or been in it. If true, he could not have gone "back" to it, as he said. A fatal slip of the tongue!

The Case of the
ATTEMPTED MURDER

"Jack Alden's account of the attempted strangling of Mrs. McHenry is pretty far-fetched," Inspector Winters told Dr. Haledjian. "Yet he passed a lie detector test.

"Alden drives a delivery truck for Best Cleaners," explained the inspector. "At five minutes before noon Tuesday he drove to the McHenry House and stopped the truck in the driveway.

"He spent about two minutes filling out his delivery reports for the morning. Then he got out with a dress and two suits.

"As he closed the cab door, he noticed his front wheels were parked on the garden hose which ran from an outlet by the garage around to the back of the house. Alden claims he got back into the truck and drove forward a few feet so that his engine was in the McHenry's empty garage.

"Here he noticed the door between the kitchen and the garage was open. He saw Mrs. McHenry lying on the floor by the stove.

"He rushed to her, he says, and was trying to revive her when Mr. McHenry came through the open door of the garage.

"McHenry had taken the day off to water his back-yard garden. He had been hosing down his flowerbeds and hedges for half an hour when he noticed the truck in his garage. He walked over to investigate.

"We can't get McHenry," concluded the inspector, "to state definitely whether he thinks Alden was trying to throttle his wife or revive her."

"No wonder the lie detector test didn't trap Alden!" said Haledjian.

Why not?

Because Alden told the truth.

Haledjian deduced that McHenry, while throttling his wife, had been surprised by the arrival of the deliveryman and had hurried to the back yard and his alibi of hosing his garden.

Had he been there all the time, he would have investigated why the water stopped flowing. The truck wheels were parked on the garden hose for "about two minutes," remember?

The Case of the
ATTIC SUICIDE

Motoring through Ashe City, Dr. Haledjian decided to drop in on his old friend, Carl Messner. At Messner's home he was shocked to learn that three days earlier his friend had hanged himself.

"Carl Messner was in excellent health and spirits when I heard from him last month," Haledjian told the sheriff. "I can't believe he committed suicide."

"He did — I investigated it myself," replied the sheriff. "Here's all there is to the case.

"Archie Carter, Mr. Messner's manservant, was returning to the house late that night when he noticed a light in the attic. As Carter got out of his car, he saw through the open attic window Mr. Messner knotting a rope around his neck. The other end of the rope was tied to a rafter. Then Mr. Messner calmly kicked away the small stool he was standing on, and that was it.

"Carter found the house doors locked. He had forgotten his key so he ran to a neighbor and telephoned me. He reported to me exactly what I've told you," said the sheriff.

"When I got out to the Messner house, I had to force the front door. Then Carter and I dashed up three floors to the attic. Mr. Messner was dead. The coroner has no doubt death was from hanging.

"The attic floor was clear except for the little stool that lay overturned by the door, and a broken clay jug that must have been hit by the stool," concluded the sheriff.

"I'd like to go out to the house again," said Haledjian. "From what you've told me of Carter's story, he's lying!"

How did Haledjian know?

Archie Carter claimed he saw Carl Messner kick a small stool from under him. However, standing on the ground, Carter could never have seen a small stool through an attic window three stories above him!

The Case of the
BALLOON MAN

"The whole force is looking for Izzy the Balloon Man who kidnaped little Dennis Farrell," Inspector Winters said to Dr. Haledjian.

"Doesn't anyone know where Izzy hangs out?"

"Nobody knows anything about him," replied the inspector. "Once a week he stops his old truck by the Farrell estate and gives out popcorn and mouse-shaped pink balloons. The kids love the funny faces he makes as he puts the balloons to his lips and huffs and puffs.

"Last Thursday Izzy made his usual stop and drove off — or so it appeared. Later, Sam Potts and the Reverend Bevin were in Sam's back yard, which abuts the Farrell property. Sam noticed one of Izzy's balloons stuck high in his oak tree.

"Since there was no wind to blow it loose, Sam got a long ladder and climbed into the tree. From that height — about twenty feet — he could see over the Farrell's twelve-foot wall.

"Sam says that as he released the balloon he glanced into the Farrell yard and saw the Balloon Man put young Dennis into his truck and drive off. He told the minister what he'd seen. Neither man thought much of it till they heard that Dennis was missing.

"Yesterday," concluded the inspector, "Dennis's father received a note stating that Dennis was being held for ransom, and that instructions would follow."

"Putting together everything you've told me," said Haledjian, "I think both Dennis and the Balloon Man have been kidnaped!"

Why?

Haledjian realized Sam Potts had used the innocent clergyman to confirm a tale of kidnaping which never occurred as he reported it.

Potts had obviously stuck the balloon high in the oak as a prop. On a day without a wind, a balloon blown up by breath could never rise high into a tree.

The Case of the
BAMBOO FENCE

"Now this here place," said the bandy-legged little guide, "is Dead Man's Creek, being so named for the tragedy in '98."

Dr. Haledjian and the other dudes on the Wild West tour gazed blankly upon a muddy stream.

"Doc Holloway's cabin stood right there," continued the guide. "I guess Doc was the most popular fellow in these parts.

"Well, one afternoon Doc is patchin' up a peddler when Jim Sterling busts in. Jim says he was in town when a lone desperado with a pair of fancy six-shooters cleaned out the bank. In all the fuss and shootin', Jim is mistaken for the gunman and has to hightail it to save his hide.

" 'The bandit done dropped one of his sixes,' says Jim. 'Iffin I ever see the mate, I'll have me the real culprit.'

"There was no time for playin' detective just

11

then. A posse was comin'. Doc believed Jim was innocent, and so he puts on Jim's shirt and hat. Doc figures to lead the posse off long enough for Jim to escape.

"After getting his patient, the peddler, to keep his mouth shut, Doc cuts a length of rail about six feet long from his bamboo fence.

He tells Jim to sit in the creek and breathe through the hollow bamboo, which is maybe as big around as a two-bit piece.

"Then Doc rides Jim's horse away, and the posse follows. Later, Jim is cleared, but it ain't no good. Jim is dead — drowned in the creek.

"The peddler fished him out an hour after Doc decoyed the posse. Doc reckoned poor Jim panicked under water and drowned."

"He didn't panic," corrected Haledjian. "He was murdered."

How did Haledjian know?

Breathing through a tube six feet long and as big around as a two-bit piece (25¢), Jim would have passed out promptly. He would have been breathing in the same air as he had just expelled — air without oxygen — a simple medical fact Doc Holloway certainly knew!

The Case of the
BIG DEAL

Dr. Haledjian had just ordered a drink at the bar in the Las Vegas motel when a lean young stranger with sun-bleached golden hair and tanned cheeks took the stool beside him.

After asking for a gin and tonic, the sunburned young man nodded toward the gaming tables. "Name's Clive Vance," he said genially. "It's sure great to be back in civilization and hear money talking out loud."

The famous sleuth introduced himself. "I take it you've been out on the desert?"

"Got back yesterday," said Vance. "Washed the dust out of my ears, had a real live barber shave off seven months of whiskers and trim this mop of wheat. Then I bought a whole wardrobe on credit. All I had to show was my assay report. Boy, am I ever ready to celebrate."

"You found gold?"

13

"Right you are. Hit pay dirt." Vance stroked his bronzed chin thoughtfully. He lowered his voice confidentially.

"Listen," he said. "If I can find a backer, I'll take enough out of those hills to buy ten pleasure palaces like this one.

"Of course," he added apologetically, "I'm not trying to interest you, doctor. Still, if you know somebody who'd like to get in on a sure thing, let me know. I'm staying in room 210. Can't give out details here, you understand."

"I understand," said Haledjian, "that you'd better improve your story if you want to part some sucker from his money."

What was wrong with Vance's story?

Vance claimed he had a barber shave off "seven months of whiskers" the day before. Yet his cheeks were "tanned" and his chin was "bronzed." Had he really been in the sun seven months without a shave, his skin would have shown white where his whiskers grew.

The Case of the
BITTER DRINK

Notwithstanding the 110-degree heat, the fifty American tourists seemed to have arrived in the Mexican village at a lucky time.

The initiation of a village youth to manhood was under way, the tour's guide announced.

A young man came jogging into the village. Sweating profusely, he sat down under a shade tree. Another villager fed him ice, wiped him dry, and massaged his neck and shoulders.

The tour's guide took a wooden cup from the local elder.

"Now comes the final test," said the guide. "The youth, having just completed a forty-mile run, must drink this cup of bitterest potion without changing expression."

The guide offered the cup to the tourists. Three men sipped it, and instantly gagged violently.

The guide talked quickly, and somehow the

Americans were making large wagers with him that the youth could not pass the drinking test.

Dr. Haledjian, one of the tourists, never took his gaze from the cup, which passed to the youth undisturbed.

The youth drained it without batting an eye.

"You and the villagers have a neat con game here," Haledjian told the guide. "But I advise you to refund all bets, or I shall notify the district police!"

How were the tourists cheated?

The taste buds of the youth's tongue had been anesthetized by the ice fed him.

The Case of the
BLACKMAILER

"I don't mind telling you, Dr. Haledjian," said Thomas Hunt, "that inheriting the Hunt millions has had its nerve-racking moments. Do you remember Martin, the gardener?"

"A smiling and bowing little chap," said Haledjian, pouring his young friend a brandy.

"That's the fellow. I dismissed him upon inheriting the house in East Hampton. Well, three days ago he came to my office, bowing and smirking, and demanded one hundred thousand dollars.

"He claimed to have been tending the spruce trees outside my father's study when Dad drew up another will, naming his brother in New Zealand sole heir."

"You believed him?"

"I confess the news hit me like a thunderbolt. Dad and I had quarreled over Veronica sometime during the last week in November. Dad opposed

17

the marriage, and it seemed plausible that he had cut me off.

"Martin asserted he possessed this second will, which he felt sure would be worth a good deal more to me than he was asking. As it was dated November 31—the day after the executed will—it would be legally recognized, he claimed.

"I refused to be blackmailed. He tried to bargain, asking fifty thousand and then twenty-five thousand."

"You paid nothing, I hope?" asked Haledjian.

"I paid—with my foot firm on the seat of his pants."

"Quite right," approved Haledjian. "Imagine trying to peddle a tale like that!"

What was Martin's blunder?

No legal will could be dated November 31, November contains only thirty days.

The Case of the
BOGUS
ROBBERY

Since she was the richest woman in New York City, Mrs. Sydney had gratified every whim but one. She had never confounded Dr. Haledjian.

So Haledjian knew the game of stump-the-detective had commenced again when at two o'clock in the morning he was summoned from the guest room of Mrs. Sydney's Fifth Avenue mansion by the butler who announced, "Madam's jewels have been stolen."

Entering Mrs. Sydney's bedroom, the famed sleuth closed the door and swiftly surveyed the scene.

The French windows were open. To the left of the disordered bed stood an end table with a book and two candles. The candles had burned down to three inches, spilling all their drippings down the side facing the door.

A bell cord lay on the thick green carpet. A drawer of the vanity table was open.

"What happened?" inquired Haledjian.

"I was reading in bed by candlelight when the door blew open," said Mrs. Sydney. "As you perhaps felt, a strong draft comes in. I pulled the bell cord for James, the butler, to come shut the door.

"Before he arrived, a masked man with a gun entered and forced me to tell him where I kept my jewels. As he scooped them into his pocket, James entered. The thief bound him with the bell cord and tied my hands and legs with these," she said, holding up a pair of stockings.

"As he departed, I asked him to have the decency to close the door. He merely laughed and deliberately left it open.

"It took James twenty minutes to work free and release me. I shall have a beastly cold in the morning!" concluded Mrs. Sydney.

"My compliments," said Haledjian, "on a nicely staged crime, with the fallacy fairly displayed."

What was the fallacy?

The candles spilled "all their drippings down the side facing the door."

Had the door really been left open as long as claimed, some wax would have dripped on the opposite side, away from the draft.

The Case of the
BROKEN ARM

"A knowledge of human behavior is often the explanation behind the criminologist's seemingly fantastic deductions," said Dr. Haledjian.

"A case in point was the murder of Roger Duffy, faked to look like suicide," said Haledjian. "Want to hear about it?"

"Can't we order dinner first?" said Octavia.

Haledjian smiled indulgently and continued.

"Duffy's body was found at 8 P.M. slumped on a park bench, a bullet in his left temple. His right arm, encased in a cast from fingertips to elbow since an accident the month before, lay on his lap. His left hand clutched a .32 pistol.

"Called to the scene and estimating that death had occurred about 7 P.M., I deduced from the contents of his pockets that he had been murdered in his bathroom and transported to the park.

"Astonishing, you gasp? Not at all. Since I real-

21

ized Duffy's clothes had been put on after his death, it seemed logical that he was undressed at the time of death. The hour pointed to an evening bath. Traces of blood in his bathroom confirmed my theory.

"Now, you ask, what was in his pockets that proved murder, not suicide? His right trouser pocket held four dollar bills clipped together and fifty-two cents in coins; his left trouser pocket had a handkerchief and cigarette lighter; his left hip pocket held his wallet.

"Surely you can see where the murderer made his mistake!" concluded Haledjian.

"Yes, killing Duffy on an empty stomach," said Octavia, filling up on water. "Who can think clearly when he's hungry? I give up."

Do you?

From the contents of Duffy's right-hand trouser pocket, Haledjian realized Duffy had not dressed himself.

With his right arm "encased in a cast from fingertips to elbow," he could not have fished into his right-hand trouser pocket. His right-side pocket would have been empty instead of containing commonly used articles such as money.

The Case of the

BRONZE NYMPH

"All the lights were out in the house last night when I heard a scuffling. I jumped out of bed to investigate and saw someone dash from my wife's room and race downstairs," Russell Evren told Inspector Winters.

"I gave chase. The intruder ran onto the back porch, where we keep a yellow insect light burning all night, and I recognized Jim Simmons."

"That's a lie!" shouted Simmons.

"Jim ran about a hundred yards," continued Evren, unruffled. "Then he threw something away. It struck several times on the rocky slope to the ravine, tracing its path in the darkness with a series of little sparks."

"Unfortunately for you, Mr. Simmons," said the inspector, "Mr. Evren was able to lead us right to the spot after he discovered his wife dead, and we found this."

The inspector held up a bronze statuette of a nymph. "Another hour and the hard rain that fell might have washed away all clues. The blood and hair found on the base match Mrs. Evren's. The lab got one good print—your forefinger."

"I wasn't near their house," protested Simmons. "Evren telephoned me early in the evening and told me he wanted to speak with me at my apartment at eight o'clock. He never showed. I stayed there until midnight, went out for a beer, and then hit the sack. As for the fingerprints, why, I handled that statuette while visiting the Evrens two days ago!"

That night the inspector told Dr. Haledjian, "Evren and Simmons are business partners who don't get along."

"Neither does Evren's attempt to frame Simmons," replied Haledjian.

Why not?

Evren claimed the "something" thrown by Simmons, which turned out to be a bronze nymph, the alleged murder weapon, struck sparks on the rocky slope, marking its path. Impossible.

Bronze, an anti-friction metal widely used in olden days for cannon, cannot strike sparks on rock.

The Case of the
BUMPED HEAD

The express train running between New York and Los Angeles had to back up outside Chicago.

Alas, the engineer stopped the train too suddenly while in reverse. Passengers tumbled like tenpins, incurring several suits against the railroad.

"The stop happened at 9 P.M.," said Mills, the railroad's insurance man, while discussing the incident with Dr. Haledjian.

Mills related the biggest headache — Ted Sheldon, a passenger who was suing for one hundred thousand dollars.

"At 8 P.M.," said Mills, "Sheldon had the porter make up his berth in the last car. He claims he had just retired for the night when the stop occurred.

"He says he was so forcefully jerked that his head struck the wall behind his pillows.

"Because of terrific head pains, he says, he left the train at Chicago," concluded Mills. He showed

Haledjian a Chicago doctor's affidavit that Sheldon had suffered a skull fracture.

"You think Sheldon hurt his head somewhere else?" asked the sleuth.

"If I can't disprove his story about his hitting his head in the Pullman berth, the company is going to have to settle."

"You won't have any trouble," said Haledjian. *Why not?*

As all Pullman berths are made up with head toward the front of the train, Sheldon, jerked by a train stopping while moving backward, would have banged his feet, not his head!

The Case of the
BURIED TREASURE

"From the gleam in your eye, I deduce you are about to get rich quick," said Dr. Haledjian.

"Clever of you, old chap," said Bertie Tilford, a young Englishman with a superiority complex toward work. "If I had a mere ten thousand I should realize a fortune! Have you ten?"

"What's the game now?" demanded Haledjian. "Pieces-of-eight among the corals? Doubloons from Kidd's chest?"

Bertie opened a sack and triumphantly produced a shining silver candlestick. "Sterling silver," he sang. "See what's engraved on the bottom."

Haledjian upended the candlestick and read the name *Lady North*. "Wasn't that the ship that sank in 1956?"

"The *Lady North* sank, but not with all hands as is generally believed," replied Bertie. "Four men

27

got away with a fortune in loot before the ship capsized in the storm.

"They hid their loot in a cave," continued Bertie. "But the storm started an avalanche and sealed off the entrance, burying three of the sailors inside. The fourth, a chap named Pembroot, escaped. Pembroot's been trying to raise ten thousand to buy the land on which the cave is located."

"You put up the money, the cave is opened, and the loot is divided two ways instead of four. Enchanting," said Haledjian. "Only how do you know Pembroot isn't a swindler?"

"Earlier tonight he took me to the cave," said Bertie. "This sack was half buried in the bushes, and I nearly sprained an ankle on it. I took one look and brought the candlestick here nonstop. You've got to agree it's the real thing, old chap."

"It is," admitted Haledjian. "And there's no doubt that Pembroot planted it by the cave for your benefit."

How did Haledjian know?

If the sterling silver candlestick had been lying in a sack since 1956, it would have been tarnished, not "shining."

The Case of the
CAVE
PAINTINGS

"By Jove! This time I'm going to make us both rich!" exclaimed Bertie Tilford, the unemployed Englishman with more get-quick-rich schemes than tail feathers on a turkey farm.

He paused dramatically, eyeing Dr. Haledjian.

"You've heard of the caveman paintings in the Cave of Font de Gaume, France?" he resumed. "Well, my associate, Sebastian Delsolo, has found the greatest ever example of prehistoric art in a cave on a farm in Spain.

"Of course," went on Bertie, "I can't divulge the exact location yet. But we can buy the farm with the cave for a mite, dear boy. The farmer suspects nothing. Think of the fortune from tourists!"

Bertie passed three photos to Haledjian. "Behold! Sebastian pushed past subterranean water channels as far down as four thousand feet to photograph those drawings!"

The first photo was of a drawing of a woolly rhinoceros, the second of hunters attacking a dinosaur, the third of a charging mammoth.

"The cave artist worked by light from a stone lamp filled with fat and fitted with a wick of moss," explained Bertie. "He used pieces of red and yellow ochre for drawing and ground them and mixed them with animal fat for painting."

"How much to buy the farm?" asked Haledjian darkly.

"In American — fifty thousand dollars," said Bertie. "But you can have a third share of everything for a mere ten thousand."

"A third of nothing, you mean," corrected Haledjian. "I won't give you a nickel!"

Why not?

The drawing of "hunters attacking a dinosaur" was obviously a fake.

Man did not appear till millions of years after the dinosaurs had died out and probably did not even suspect their existence.

The Case of the
DEAD BOXER

Tony Cerone's worldly possessions were laid out on a small table in police headquarters. They consisted of a T-shirt, sneakers, and white cotton trousers. In a pocket of the trousers was a card.

The card read: July 28. Your wght, 173 lbs.; Your fortune, You will enjoy a long life.

"His life lasted 22 years," Inspector Winters told Dr. Haledjian.

"Late last night," said the inspector, "we got a call to come to the carnival. Somebody had started up a Ferris wheel. We found a male corpse jack-knifed over a strut. At first I thought the guy had been beaten to death—his face was so battered. Then I recognized Tony.

"Last night Tony fought Kirby Malone for the state middleweight title," he continued. "Tony took a pounding. We know he left the arena still pretty dazed. He must have come out to the carnival. He used to be a roustabout, and he knew his way around.

"It looks like he got here after closing," said the inspector, "used the scale, and then started up the big wheel. He took a ride and fell out. The medical examiner says he died instantly."

The famed criminologist contemplated Tony's possessions.

"He might have been killed elsewhere and hung on the strut," said Haledjian. "I heard rumors of a fix in the Malone fight.

"It looks to me like Tony refused to take a dive and the mob made him pay the full price. The killers apparently did a clumsy job. To avoid giving themselves away, they changed his clothes and staged the scene out at the Ferris wheel."

How did Haledjian know?

Tony could not have gained 13 pounds in a day. He fought on the night of his death for the state middleweight — 160 pounds — title. When found, he had on someone else's clothing, for the card in his pocket gave his body weight as an impossible "173 lbs."

The Case of the
COIN
COLLECTOR

Death, Dr. Haledjian ascertained quickly, had been inflicted by a blunt instrument within the past half hour.

He carefully rolled the body of his old friend, Hugh Clark, on its back. Something glinted within the red carnation in Clark's lapel. Haledjian recognized the object instantly — a gold stater of Croesus — a rare coin.

The sleuth replaced the coin in the carnation, rolled the body to its original position lying face down on the floor, and thoughtfully regarded the pockets, which were all turned inside out.

He was examining the kitchen of the dead man's three-room bachelor apartment when Clark's nephew, Jim Mimms, entered.

"Uncle Hugh is lying dead in the living room! What happened, Dr. Haledjian?" cried the young man.

Haledjian handed Mimms an open canister of flour to hold while he picked out the one marked tea.

"Your uncle," he said to Mimms, "telephoned me this morning and asked me to come right over. He was planning to take a rare coin downtown for sale and wanted me along. Apparently somebody arrived first—I found the door open—and slugged your uncle to death. The killer searched the body but found nothing, because your uncle didn't put the coin in his pocket!"

Haledjian paused to set a kettle of water on the stove. "You might bring the coin to me. It's buried in the flower."

Young Mimms put down the canister he was holding and left the kitchen. In a moment he was back with the coin, taken from the carnation.

"How deeply are you mixed up in this murder?" snapped Haledjian.

How come?

Mimms proved he was involved by taking the coin from the carnation, which he couldn't see because the body was "lying face down on the floor." Had he been innocent, he would have assumed when Haledjian said the coin was "buried in the flower" that it was buried in the flour—in the canister of flour he was holding.

The Case of the
DEAD BROKER

The corpse of Winthrop Parida sat facing the ocean on the deserted northern end of the boardwalk at Leedo Beach, slumped to the right against the arm of the stone bench.

From the bullet wound in the center of the forehead dried blood descended in a solid line down the right side of the face, staining his white collar and blue-dotted gold tie.

"A trash collector discovered the body at eight this morning," Inspector Winters told Dr. Haledjian.

"Death occurred between midnight and two this morning," said Haledjian. He studied the pistol on the boardwalk. "You're convinced it's suicide?"

"Parida's been despondent over the recent failure of his brokerage firm," replied the inspector. "Last night he attended a party. Afterward, the whole group drove out here in several cars to eat hot dogs at Benny's.

"It turned cold and a windstorm arose that didn't let up till dawn. Around 11 P.M. Parida excused himself and went outdoors. His friends got worried about him, but after waiting till 1 A.M., they figured he had gone home alone in his car. So they all returned to the city about 2 A.M.

"This wasn't the first time Parida had moodily walked out of a party in the past few weeks," concluded the inspector. "But nobody suspected he'd ever take his own life."

"He didn't," said Haledjian.

How did Haledjian know?

Had Parida shot himself on the bench during the windstorm, the blood from the wound would not have "descended in a solid line" down his face. The wind would have smeared it over his face and spattered it on his clothing.

Hence, Haledjian knew he was killed somewhere else and the suicide faked.

The Case of the
DEAD
FRENCHMAN

The body of Yves du Motier was found in the bedroom of the apartment belonging to Silas Howe, the coin collector.

Du Motier had been stabbed to death with a letter opener. The body lay four feet from the rumpled bed.

"Death occurred about 8:30 A.M., or half an hour before the body was discovered," Inspector Winters told Dr. Haledjian.

"I telephoned Silas Howe, who has been in Philadelphia attending a numismatics convention. He says that last month he brought du Motier, a French coin collector and an old friend, from France for an operation to restore du Motier's hearing.

"The way it looks, somebody used a skeleton key to get into Howe's apartment and tried to steal his rare coins. Du Motier must have awakened, seen the intruder, and in the struggle was slain. The safe where Howe keeps his coins was unopened. No coins are missing as far as we can tell."

"Who notified the police?" inquired Haledjian.

"James Wilkes, a neighbor in the apartment house. Wilkes was on his way to work when he saw Howe's door open, and hearing the alarm clock ringing, investigated. He found the Frenchman dead on the floor."

"When did Howe leave for Philadelphia, and who can verify his presence there?" asked Haledjian.

"He left three days ago," said the inspector. "We contacted his hotel manager, who swears Howe was in and out on each of the past three days. Say —I see what you're getting at!"

Whom did Haledjian suspect?

Wilkes—who claimed to have been attracted by the ringing of the alarm clock—a fatal slip, since du Motier who was deaf would not have set the alarm.

The Case of the
DEAD JUDGE

"Who are you?" demanded Dr. Haledjian of the sallow stranger who answered the doorbell at Judge Casper's residence.

"I'm Bernard Mitchell, Judge Casper's new law clerk," was the blurted answer. "The judge just killed himself!"

The sallow man led Haledjian into the den. Judge Casper lay slumped across his desk. Gripped in his left hand was a .32 revolver. His right hand rested on the desk beside a note.

Dr. Haledjian read:

"Since giving Arthur Brennet a suspended sentence, I have been the target of a defaming whispering campaign. I do not have the strength to keep asserting that I was not bought off. Were I younger, I should fight this libel. But for that I do not possess enough strength."

Said Mitchell, "The judge had been under attack

39

since he let off Brennet, the influence peddler, so lightly last year. Somebody started rumors that he'd been bribed. The remarks were libelous, and I kept urging him to sue. But he said he was too old for a fight."

Haledjian completed his examination of the bullet wound. "He's been dead only a few minutes. Did you hear a shot?"

"Yes, I dashed in here and found him already dead."

"How long have you been the judge's law clerk?"

"Only a week."

"Well, you'd better come with me to the police," said Haledjian. "They'll want to hear your alibi."

Why did Haledjian suspect Mitchell?

Haledjian knew Mitchell wasn't a law clerk. He and the judge's suicide note misused an elementary legal term to describe the defaming rumors — "libel" (published statement) instead of the proper word, "slander" (spoken statement).

The Case of the
DEAD
MILLIONAIRE

"I see Willie Van Swelte just reached his twenty-first birthday," said Inspector Winters, looking up from his newspaper. "Tomorrow he gets the ten million his father left him."

"Didn't the old man commit suicide twenty years ago?" asked Dr. Haledjian.

"Yes," replied the inspector. "And there was always something that puzzled me about the case. Edgar Van Swelte shot himself below the heart. The bullet passed upward, piercing the heart all right. Death was instantaneous. But why did he aim like that — upward?

"Another thing — no suicide note. Nobody was in the house when he died. I've got a picture of the scene, though."

The inspector drew from his files a manila folder and picked out a glossy print. It showed Edgar Van Swelte dead. His body, seated in the kitchen,

41

had fallen across the kitchen table. His right hand, still clutching the gun, rested on the table close beside the back of his head.

"The cook discovered the body upon returning from the market," continued the inspector. "She claims she telephoned the police promptly. When our photographer snapped this, it was 1 A.M. Edgar had been dead approximately six hours."

Haledjian studied the twenty-year-old photograph. Then he inquired, "How tall was Edgar?"

"Five-feet-eight, but long-legged, so that when he sat down, he appeared much shorter," answered the inspector.

"Then I should say there can be no doubt that he was murdered," announced Haledjian.

How did Haledjian reach his conclusion?

Had Van Swelte shot himself "from below the heart" while seated, he must have held the gun close to his lap. Since death was "instantaneous," it would have been impossible for him, a short-bodied man, to have lifted the hand with the gun until it "rested on the table" after shooting himself.

The Case of the
DEAD PROFESSOR

"I heard a shot as I was sorting the silverware," said Mrs. Grummand, the housekeeper. "When I entered the study, Professor Townsend was li — like that!"

Seated at his desk was Reingald Townsend, chairman of the English Department of Overton University.

Haledjian studied the position of the body, which had sagged against the left arm of the leather swivel chair. The bullet had entered the right temple. A .38 caliber, double-action 1875 Army revolver lay in Townsend's lap.

On the desk was a note apparently signed by Reingald Townsend. Haledjian read:

"After having spoken with Dinker this morning, I have decided not to delay. I do what I must. Not even you, dearest Kay, can know the bottomless despair of being compelled to retire. Too old! To

43

fully understand, one must have taught thirty-five years, as I have. Ahead is nothing. Farewell, I love you."

"Who are Dinker and Kay?" inquired Haledjian.

"Dinker is Paul Dinkerton, president of the university," replied the housekeeper. "Kay is Mrs. Townsend. She was called out of town suddenly. She left about ten this morning."

"Who are Professor Townsend's heirs?"

Mrs. Grummand hesitated. "Why, it is generally believed that Mrs. Townsend and I will share equally."

"Even if Professor Townsend was murdered?"

Why did Haledjian reject suicide?

The suicide note was an obvious phony. The chairman of the English Department would never have committed two grammatical sins—a redundant phrase and a split infinitive.

He would have written, "Having spoken," instead of "After having spoken," and "To understand fully," instead of "To fully understand."

The Case of
DEATH AT SUNRISE

Inspector Winters raised the tattered window shade, letting morning light into the dingy room of Nick the Nose.

In the courtyard four stories below, policemen were gathered around the shattered body of a young woman.

"Let's hear it again," the inspector said to Nick.

Nick, who hadn't sold one of his phony tips to the police in months, shifted nervously.

"About sunrise I'm sitting in this chair reading the racing form," began the greasy little informer. "I got the insomnia, see? Suddenly I hear scuffling, and I see Mrs. Clark. She lives right across the court on the fourth floor.

"Well, she's struggling with a man in a uniform. He gives her a shove toward the window, and whammy, out she goes!

"The first thing I think of is you — maybe you'll

figure it's suicide instead of murder. So I run down to the drugstore and telephone you. I stayed with the body till we came up here, just to keep everything like it was for you."

Nick licked his lips. "I seen the killer's face. I figure I can identify him or at least tell you what kind of uniform he had on. That ought to be worth something."

"It is — this!" growled the inspector, delivering his foot to the seat of Nick's pants.

"Quite the appropriate payment," commented Haledjian when he heard of Nick's latest attempt at a payday.

Why did Nick get the boot instead of cash?

The inspector surmised that Nick had discovered the body while entering the building and concocted the murder angle for a buck.

He couldn't have seen from the window of his room what he described. The shade was drawn, remember?

The Case of the
DEATH PLUNGE

While browsing in the Professional Photographers' Exhibition, Dr. Haledjian stopped to admire a striking photograph in the flashgun category entitled "Death Plunge."

The print showed a small girl touching a lighted match to a Christmas candle. Beside the candle stood a pile of gifts. The girl was blonde, pugnosed, adorable.

But what made the photograph spellbinding was the second figure.

It was a woman, back to camera, falling past the picture window just behind the little girl.

The caption read:

"This remarkable shot was taken August 24 at 9:30 P.M. by Bertram Kennedy in his Brooklyn studio apartment. At the moment Mr. Kennedy took the picture, Mrs. Claire Gramelin was falling from the roof six stories above. Her body, stopped in midair, produced this startling backdrop for what was intended as the Christmas cover of *Family Times Magazine*. It is believed Mrs. Gramelin, who weighed only ninety pounds, lost her footing in the storm winds which reached forty miles an hour that night. She died upon striking the sidewalk."

Haledjian finished reading as a group of officials moved in his direction. One of the men held a blue ribbon. As he was about to pin it to "Death Plunge," Haledjian spoke up.

"I wouldn't do that," cautioned the famed sleuth. "Unless you want to award first prize to an obvious fake!"

How did Haledjian know?

The picture window was closed, or else the little girl could not have held a lighted match in winds of "forty miles an hour." Therefore, the body of the woman could not have been seen falling outside. Remember, the shot was snapped at night with a flashgun, making the room brighter than the outdoors; thus, the window would have acted as a mirror, reflecting the room rather than transmitting the figure of Mrs. Gramelin.

The Case of the
DENTIST'S PATIENT

Dr. Evelyn Williams, London-born New York dentist, was preparing to take a wax impression of the right lower teeth of his patient, Dorothy Hoover. Silently the door behind him opened. A gloved hand holding an automatic appeared.

Two shots sounded. Miss Hoover slumped over, dead.

"We've got a suspect," Inspector Winters told Dr. Haledjian at his office an hour afterward. "The elevator boy took a nervous man to the fifteenth floor — Dr. Williams has one of six offices on the floor — a few moments before the shooting. The description fits John 'Torpedo' Burton.

"Burton is out on parole," continued the inspector. "I had him picked up at his rooming house. As far as he knows, I want to question him about a minor parole infraction."

Burton was ushered in and angrily demanded,

"What's this all about?"

"Ever hear of Dr. Evelyn Williams?" asked the inspector.

"No, why?"

"Dorothy Hoover was shot to death less than two hours ago as she sat in a chair in Dr. Williams' office."

"I been sleeping all afternoon."

"An elevator operator says he took a man answering your description to the fifteenth floor a moment before the shots."

"It wasn't me," snarled Burton. "I look like a lot of guys. I ain't been near a dentist's office since Sing Sing. This Williams, I bet he never saw me, so what can you prove?"

"Enough," snapped Dr. Haledjian, "to send you to the chair!"

What was the basis of Haledjian's remark?

Although Burton claimed never to have heard of a Dr. Evelyn Williams, he knew the doctor was (1) a dentist, and (2) a man.

50

The Case of
FLAWLESS PHIL

"I've caught a good many crooks, but I've never tried to catch one while posing as a used-car salesman," confessed Dr. Haledjian.

"We think one of the men who have been smuggling dope across the border will be around for that car," replied Sheriff Monahan.

He pointed to a 1954 gray sedan. "Last week we got a tip that dope was being smuggled in a car parked outside Priestly's Bar & Grille. We missed the smugglers, but got the car. Under the back seat we found a million dollars worth of pure heroin.

"We had to rip up the entire floor of the car to get the stuff," went on the sheriff. "Phil Barton, who runs this car lot as Phil's Flawless Finds, agreed to put the car on display. It's bait. We hope the smugglers will try to find out if the dope is still hidden in it."

Haledjian agreed to play the part of a salesman. On the windshield he stuck a poster that announced: Phil's Flawless Special Today Only.

After a while a dark-haired man moved toward the sedan.

"May I help you?" inquired Haledjian, and began his sales pitch. The customer edged toward the sedan without ever getting nearer than six feet of it. He seemed only halfheartedly interested as he peered at the engine.

Haledjian stepped around to the driver's window. "The engine has only twelve thousand miles on it. The inside," he admitted, "is floorless."

"Is it?" said the man, and walked hurriedly away.

"He's one of the smugglers," shouted Haledjian. "Arrest him!"

How did Haledjian know?

The man was scared off because he thought Haledjian said the car was "floorless," which in fact Haledjian did say.

But as the man never got close enough to see the floor of the car, he would have assumed, had he not been floor-minded, that Haledjian had said "flawless," the slogan of the car lot.

The Case of the
FOOTPRINT

Half a mile from where the body of Art Sikes, a hunter, had been found stabbed to death, was a rudely constructed hut.

The occupant, an eccentric hermit who grubbed a meager living from the surrounding forest by hunting and fishing, was the only human being found within thirty miles of the murder.

He was taken into custody protesting his innocence.

The local police chief established the following facts as the "wild man" crouched miserably in his jail cell grunting, "No kill man."

(1) Sikes had been stabbed two days before, or about the time the heavy rains had stopped.

(2) Since then an unseasonable heat wave had gripped the area, baking the ground dry.

Hearing that Dr. Haledjian was nearby, the police chief summoned the sleuth to show off his up-to-date, scientific police methods.

"This morning we got the big break," said the chief. "We found a perfect right shoe print in the clay near the scene of the crime.

"We took a plaster impression," continued the chief. "It's the exact size and shape of that crazy man's new shoe."

Haledjian obtained permission to examine the suspect's shoes.

"His shoes are new, all right," said Haledjian, "but of a kind sold by the hundreds to trappers and hunters. I'm afraid, chief, your plastic impression does more to prove him innocent than guilty."

How come?

To be the killer's, the footprint had to be made when the earth was wet, but the impression was taken after the earth had been baked dry. As earth contracts in drying, shrinking footprints up to half an inch, the fact that the undersized print (made when the ground was baked dry) fit the suspect's shoe perfectly proved it was not made by him.

The Case of
FREDDIE THE FORGER

"Somebody tipped Freddie the Forger," Inspector Winters told Dr. Haledjian. "Freddie cleared out of his hotel room an hour before we raided it."

The inspector handed Haledjian a cardboard onto which a torn sheet of paper showing dates and places had been pasted together.

"We found the pieces in Freddie's wastepaper basket," the inspector said. "So at least we know where he's going."

Haledjian read the penciled notes: Paris, Aug. 14 . . . Naples, Sept. 12 . . . Athens, Sept. 21 . . . London, Oct. 3 . . . Palestine, Oct. 15 . . . Moscow, Dec. 24.

"Looks like an itinerary," agreed Haledjian. "But is it Freddie's?"

"Toby Kirk, Freddie's New York girl, insists it's his writing. She said she was in his hotel and overheard him making a long distance telephone call.

"He talked to Paris and got a hotel reservation for August 15. She didn't overhear much, but she thinks he then made a plane reservation for a flight that left New York at 2 P.M. August 14.

"Freddie's a smart operator," continued the inspector. "He always dreams up a new disguise. Toby Kirk says when he was in New York he bought a ten-gallon hat.

"I put Diehl, my best man, on the case. Diehl leaves tonight for France. If Freddie shows up in Paris wearing a fez, Diehl will spot him and bring him back."

"Unfortunately," said Haledjian, "Diehl will be flying in the wrong direction to capture Freddie."

How come?

The fact that Freddie wrote down Palestine instead of Israel as a destination told Haledjian he planned a transcontinental flight, not a transatlantic one. The new ten-gallon hat pinpointed Texas. Paris, Naples, Athens, London, Palestine, and Moscow are all towns in the Lone Star state.

56

The Case of the
FRENCH VINEYARD

The dinner at the mansion rented by Pierre Gibrault was superb.

While the roast was being served, Gibrault arose, deftly unscrewed the cork from a chilled bottle of red table wine, and poured a little into the glass of Dr. Haledjian.

Haledjian sipped and politely nodded approval.

As Gibrault poured for his other guests, Jim Morgan, seated by Haledjian, whispered, "What do you think?"

"About the wine?" said Haledjian. "It's excellent!"

"You know, of course, why we were invited?"

"I expect Gibrault needs money," replied the sleuth.

"He was in my office last week," said Morgan, "to get a list of people who might be interested in investing in a French vineyard.

"Gibrault claims to be a wine exporter from Bordeaux, but I haven't had time to check him out," continued Morgan. "He assured me the vineyard up for sale has the richest soil in France. It produces the very best grapes. He wants to make red sparkling Burgundy to sell in America at top prices."

"How much cash does he need in a hurry?" asked Haledjian.

"The vineyard's owner wants the equivalent of a million American dollars, and he wants it by Tuesday or no sale," said Morgain. "I put your name on the guest list because I thought you might help me get a quick appraisal of Gibrault."

"I have," replied Haledjian. "Don't invest a penny!"

Why not?

Haledjian knew Gibrault was a confidence man, not a wine expert from Bordeaux because: (1) he served chilled red wine opened at the table when red table wine should be opened an hour before serving and kept at room temperature; (2) "the richest soil" does not produce the best grapes for wine; (3) the poorest, not the best, French grapes go into red sparkling Burgundy.

The Case of the
GREEN PEN

Except for the ambulance attendants, Sheriff Monahan, and Dr. Haledjian there was nobody at the Meadowbrook Bowling Lanes, the only alleys in town, except a young woman sprawled by the front door with a knife in her back.

"The lanes closed at midnight," said the sheriff. "One of my men discovered the body at 4 A.M., and I called you right away."

"Dead about an hour," said Haledjian. "Who was she?"

"Roberta Layne," replied the sheriff. "She just married Theodore Layne, a merchant captain, before he sailed for Hawaii last week. They have a little house on Bleaker Street."

"Any suspects?"

"Charlie Barnett — maybe. Roberta jilted him for Ted."

Haledjian dropped a green fountain pen by the door. "Let's pay Mr. Barnett a visit."

The suspect lived in a room behind the gasoline station he owned.

Haledjian's first words were, "Do you know Roberta has been murdered?"

"No!" gasped Barnett.

"Well, that's enough for now," said Haledjian. Then, as if in afterthought, he added, "I must have dropped my fountain pen by the front door of the lanes where we found the body. I'm due in the city in an hour. Mind getting the pen for me and leaving it with the sheriff this morning?"

Barnett looked uncertain. He shrugged. "Sure."

When he brought the pen to the sheriff's office later that morning he was promptly arrested.

Why?

Although Barnett claimed he did not know Roberta Layne had just been murdered, he knew, as Haledjian said, that the pen lay "by the front door of the lanes." Had he been innocent, he would have looked for the pen at the front door of the Laynes — that is, at their house.

The Case of the
HAUNTED HOUSE

"You can't rent more for your money than this house," said Tilford, the real estate agent. "It has charm, fancy brickwork, half-timbering, casement windows, three terraces, and a lady ghost."

"Ghost?" inquired Dr. Haledjian, pushing open a bedroom window. He gazed upon the flagstone terrace two stories below.

"The ghost is Jennifer Godley," explained Tilford. "This was her house. On March 28, 1949, she was hurled from this very window. Her body was found on the stones below.

"At first the police thought she was a suicide, or had accidentally fallen," continued Tilford. "They then realized that this window was closed when she was found.

"Henry Godley, her husband, admitted entering the bedroom and closing the window himself. It was a chilly day, and he claimed that he didn't know his wife lay dead on the stones below. Of course, he was sentenced to life — "

"Whoa!" cried Haledjian. "On what evidence?"

"Ben Taylor, a school teacher, saw the whole thing. He was out bird-watching. The Godleys lived like hermits — never had visitors, didn't allow anyone within a mile of the place. But Ben Taylor had binoculars, and at the trial he testified that he saw Henry Godley slide up the window and throw poor Jennifer head first to the terrace."

Haledjian pursed his lips in thought. The next day he telephoned Tilford.

"I've decided not to rent the house for the summer," he said. "But I'm going to see that Henry Godley is given a new trial!"

Why?

Ben Taylor lied in testifying he saw Godley "slide up" the window by which he allegedly threw his wife to her death.

It was a casement window, which is hinged, and which Haledjian opened by "pushing."

The Case of the
HERO DOG

"My pitch last night was beautiful," Cyril Makin, the woeful wooer, told Dr. Haledjian. "How did Trudy Shore ever see through it?

"For three generations," continued Makin, "Trudy's family have been circus people doing a dog act. If you aren't a canine connoisseur with a fabulous dog somewhere in the family, she won't date you twice. So to score with her, I made up a grandpa and his faithful four-legged helper."

Makin sipped his drink disconsolately. Then he recounted his latest unsuccessful pitch.

"Near Grandpa's farm the railroad tracks made a hairpin turn between two stony cliffs. From his fields, Grandpa could see the tracks. If rocks fell upon them, Grandpa climbed a hill and warned the engineer by waving a red flag.

"One day Grandpa saw rocks falling on the tracks. He started for the hill as a train approached, but tripped and knocked himself unconscious. That's when the dog proved his mettle.

"The dog raced to the house. The dog pulled down Grandpa's long red underwear from the clothesline, raced to the hill, and there ran back and forth, trailing the red underwear like a warning flag.

"The engineer saw the red signal and stopped the train, saving hundreds of passengers from death or injury!" concluded Makin.

"You're lucky," said Haledjian, "Trudy didn't bite your nose off for a dog story like that!"

What was wrong with it?

Unfortunately for Cyril's pitch, the dog couldn't have known that the flag Grandpa waved was red, or that the underwear was red.
Dogs are color-blind.

The Case of the
HIDDEN
DIAMOND

The thieves spent six hours in the home of Ted Duda.

At first they searched the house, trying to find where he hid his huge diamond, valued at half a million dollars.

Then they tried beating the information out of him. They fled at dawn, fearing detection.

Fatally hurt, Duda crawled to his desk and typed a note to his partner, John Madden.

It read:

"John — four men tried to make me tell where I had hidden the diamond. At first they searched the house, raving like madmen. Then, in desperation, the barbarians split open the cat! When all failed, they beat me, but I did not tell. I'm dying. The diamond is hidden in the vane."

"Duda died this morning," Inspector Winters

told Dr. Haldejian. "We have his murderers, but not the diamond."

The inspector handed Haledjian a copy of the death note. "We took down the weathervane, a cock, but there wasn't anything inside it," the inspector said. "We're still searching the house."

Haledjian read the note and said, "You also failed to find the body of the cat, but you did find a broken barrel of liquor."

"Why, yes," said the inspector. "The thieves were thorough. They broke the barrel and every bottle in Duda's little wine cellar."

"How many walking sticks did Duda own?" The inspector looked puzzled. "One."

"It must be hollow," said Haledjian. "You'll find the diamond inside it."

The inspector did. But how did Haledjian know?

Haledjian realized that the dying Duda could not have typed errorlessly, as it appeared. He quickly saw that Duda had interchanged the "v" and "c" which are positioned next to each other on the typewriter keyboard.
Reread the note, substituting the "v" for the "c," and vice versa.

The Case of the

HITCHHIKER

"Boy, thanks for the lift," exclaimed the young man as he slid off his knapsack and climbed into the front seat of the air-conditioned patrol car beside Sheriff Monahan. "Say, aren't you going to arrest me for bumming a ride?"

"Not today," replied the sheriff. "Too busy."

The young man grinned in relief! He took a chocolate bar from his knapsack, broke off a piece, and offered the rest to the sheriff.

"No, thanks," said the police officer, accelerating the car.

"You chasing someone?" asked the hitchhiker.

"Four men just held up the First National Bank. They escaped in a big black sedan."

"Hey," gasped the hitchhiker. "I saw a black sedan about ten minutes ago. It had four men in it. They nearly ran me off the road. First car I saw in an hour. But they took a left turn. They're headed west, not north!"

Sheriff Monahan braked the patrol car and swung it around. The young man began peeling an orange, putting the rinds tidily into a paper bag.

"Look at the heat shining off the road ahead," said the sheriff. "Must be eighty-five in the shade today."

"Must be," agreed the hitchhiker. "Wait — you passed the turn off — where're you going?"

"To the police station," snapped the sheriff — a decision to which Haledjian heartily agreed upon hearing the hitchhiker's story.

How come?

The hitchhiker quickly confessed to being one of the hold-up gang, left behind to misdirect pursuit. His story was obviously phony, since he "broke off a piece" of chocolate. Standing for more than an hour in eighty-five-degree heat, as he claimed, the chocolate bar would have been soupy.

The Case of the
HOME BAKERY

"I was driving by when I got the darndest attack of indigestion," said Sheriff Monahan apologetically. "Do you have some bicarbonate of soda?"

Mrs. Duffy, a motherly woman of sixty, smiled cheerfully. "You just sit right down in the kitchen, Sheriff," she said. "I don't keep bicarbonate of soda on hand, but I'll brew you a nice cup of tea. It'll work wonders, I promise."

Sheriff Monahan seated himself obediently while Mrs. Duffy bustled about her neat little kitchen. He had always admired the kindly woman who dwelt alone and made her own living.

After the sheriff had finished his tea, he rose to leave. "I feel better already. Many thanks."

Outside, he saw Mrs. Duffy's panel truck. It was parked by the south wing of the house which, he had always assumed, was her bakery, in which she made the bread, cakes, and pies she sold to inns along the highway.

He studied the pink lettering on the truck: "Ma Duffy's Homemade . Pies, Cakes, and Bread." He stared thoughtfully at the house.

Back in town he telephoned Dr. Haledjian. The famed criminologist heartily advised him to get a search warrant, and within the hour the sheriff had returned to Mrs. Duffy's.

A search of the premises disclosed that Ma Duffy's pies, cakes, and bread were commercial products with wrappers removed. But the bottles of whiskey illegally secreted within each pullman loaf were strictly home brewed.

What made the sheriff suspicious?

The sheriff realized that Mrs. Duffy wasn't baking in the back of her house when she said, "I don't keep bicarbonate of soda on hand." Bicarbonate of soda is another term for baking soda, which anyone doing baking would stock as a staple.

The Case of the
HOTEL MURDER

Dr. Haledjian was shaving in his hotel room on the second floor when he heard a woman screaming, "Help!"

Tossing on his robe, he dashed into the hall. In front of room 213 a woman stood crying and screaming.

Introducing himself, Haledjian looked through the open door and saw a man slumped in an easy chair. A swift examination showed he had just been killed by a bullet through the heart.

"Try to get hold of yourself and tell me what happened," said the sleuth.

"I'm Clara Uffner," sobbed the woman. "A few moments ago I heard a knock on the door. A voice said, 'Telegram.'

"I opened the door. A masked man stood there, a gun in his gloved hand. He shot my husband, tossed the gun into the room, and ran."

The automatic pistol on the floor, Halejian saw, was equipped with a silencer. Returning to the hall, he noted the door at one end marked Exit.

Reentering the room, he stepped on something hard. It turned out to be an empty cartridge shell. Farther to the left was another. Both were of the caliber to match the pistol.

Embedded in the wall, about two feet above the seated body, Haledjian discovered a second bullet.

"All right, Mrs. Uffner," he said sternly. "Now tell me the truth!"

Why did he doubt Mrs. Uffner?

Had the mysterious killer fired from the hall into the room, the shells from his gun would not have fallen forward into the room and to the left. An automatic pistol ejects to the right and a few feet behind the shooter.

The Case of the

HUNTING ACCIDENT

Dr. Haledjian's weekend hunting trip ended abruptly when he stumbled upon the body of a middle-aged man dressed in hunter's garb lying in a shallow gorge.

An autopsy disclosed that death had been instantaneous. A bullet had entered just above the hip and lodged in the heart.

Investigation by the police established the dead man as John C. Mills, a New York City ad man. Further, Mills and a friend, Whit Kearns, had rented a hunting lodge near where the body was found.

Kearns was immediately brought in for questioning.

A suave, impeccably tailored sportsman of fifty, Kearns looked from the inspector to Dr. Haledjian before saying resignedly, "All right. I didn't mean to run away. I suppose I just panicked.

"Johnny Mills and I rent the same lodge every year," continued Kearns. "We've never failed to bring back one bear at least.

"We had spent a week in the woods and our time was up. It was the last day, and for the first time we hadn't shot a solitary bruin. I noticed a rock formation and climbed to the top to see if I couldn't spot one.

"Suddenly I heard John shout in terror in the clearing below me. A bear had got to him. I shot, but only wounded the bear. It reared on its hind legs. Just as I fired again, John got in the way. My bullet struck him, and he tumbled into the gorge.

"The bear disappeared," concluded Kearns. "I panicked, I admit, but I swear it was an accident!"

"The facts," said Haledjian quietly, "disprove your tale."

What was Kearns' slip?

74

Shooting into "the clearing below" from atop a rock formation, Kearns' bullet would have followed a downward angle. But the bullet that killed Mills traveled upward—from hip to heart.

The Case of the
INDIAN JUG

The day before the big Tech vs. State football game, the State mascot, an Indian jug, disappeared.

Three hours before kickoff, one of the State fraternities was anonymously informed that the jug was buried on the estate of E. B. Van Snite, millionaire Tech grad, fanatical football booster, and notorious prankster.

Six State undergraduates enlisted the aid of Dr. Haledjian. Arming them with shovels, the famous sleuth drove out to see Van Snite, an old friend.

"Certainly the jug is buried here," Van Snite said, his eyes twinkling mischievously.

The State boys gazed with dismay upon the area of ground Van Snite had indicated.

It was a freshly turned half acre, scraped and rolled and freshly sown on every inch with grass seed.

The area was walled on three sides, and a stone

walk bordered the fourth. In dead center stood a bird bath. A maple tree grew at one end of the expanse and two wild olive trees at the opposite end.

"You have two hours till kickoff," said Van Snite. The jug is hidden in the only reasonable place in the half acre.

"Find it, and you can have it back. But if you fail by game time, you must pay for planting the whole lawn."

The State boys prepared to leave. But within half an hour they had unearthed the Indian jug—after Haledjian had told them where to dig.

Where?

"The only reasonable place" was where Van Snite didn't expect to grow a lawn anyway.

That meant under the maple, whose surface roots steal food and moisture from the smaller grass roots, making grass impossible.

The Case of the
INDIAN TRADER

Dr. Haledjian and the rest of the saddle-sore dudes on the deluxe tour of western sites entered the adobe museum and stared at an empty green-tinted glass bottle.

Its label read: Doc Henry's Secret Elixir.

The tour's bandy-legged little guide recounted the reason for the bottle's enshrinement.

"Beautiful Jinny Knox was saved by seventy-seven of them bottles back in '83," he began.

"Ol' Doc Henry was an Injun trader — never sold a drop of his elixir to a white man, only to them Injuns. 'Course, Doc kept the ingredients a secret. But on his deathbed, he's supposed to have admitted it weren't nothin' but sugar water.

"Well, one night some crazy drunk Injuns kidnaped young Jinny. It was Doc Henry who volunteered to go after her.

"He set off with a wagonload of tradin' goods

and eighty bottles of his elixir hung from the beams. For five days of sub-freezin' weather he palavered with them savages.

"But Doc brings Jinny home safe. He'd had to trade all his bottles but three fer her, and all his other stuff in the bargain.

"Doc," concluded the guide, "was a hero. Imagine goin' up into them hills alone and tradin' a pack of crazy-drunk redskins out of a beautiful girl!"

"Doc was no hero," corrected Haledjian. "He was an old rascal who was partly responsible for Jinny's kidnaping!"

How did Haledjian know?

After "five days of sub-freezin' weather" the "sugar water" would have frozen and broken the glass bottles. Hence the elixir had to be something with a low freezing point — an alcoholic beverage that got the Indians "crazy drunk."

The Case of the
LAST MORENO

"From the smirk connecting your ears, I assume you've hit upon a new scheme for making a million dollars," Dr. Haledjian said to Bertie Tilford.

"Not quite a million," corrected Bertie, a young Englishman with more ways to avoid work than aces up the sleeve of a Mississippi gambler.

Bertie opened his briefcase and showed Haledjian a pen and ink sketch of a bearded man.

"Looks like a Tassado Moreno!" Haledjian marveled.

"Precisely," gloated Bertie. "All the world knows the great artist died in Alaska three years ago. The details were never divulged till his friend, Kiako, meeting hard times, came to me.

"The facts are," continued Bertie, "that Moreno injured his hip in a storm that buried his and Kiako's supplies on the trail. The weather had been

79

far below freezing for days, and Moreno, his hip injured, failed rapidly.

"Kiako got him to an abandoned shack. He stopped up the broken window with his gloves. As he tore apart a chair to build a fire, Moreno called to him. There was no time. He wouldn't live half an hour.

"Moreno asked for drawing materials. Kiako found an old pen and a bottle of ink in a cupboard. Moreno sketched his faithful friend, and died.

"The prices of Morenos have soared since his death. His last picture should be worth a quarter of a million. I can buy it from Kiako for twenty thousand," concluded Bertie. "Have you twenty, old boy?"

"For that portrait? Not twenty cents!" snapped Haledjian.

Why not?

As "the weather had been below freezing for days," and the shack had a "broken window," the ink would have been frozen solid and impossible to draw with.

The Case of the
LAZY
MURDERER

According to the coroner's report, Mrs. Treddor, the town recluse, had been bludgeoned to death two days ago in the kitchen of her decaying hill-top mansion.

"I received an anonymous telephone call at 4 A.M. yesterday that she had been murdered," Sheriff Monahan confessed to Dr. Haledjian. "Heaven help me, I thought it was just another prank and didn't investigate till this afternoon!

"Living alone, never showing herself anywhere, why Mrs. Treddor's been the butt of every practical joke in the book, including the death gimmick, a dozen times."

The sheriff conducted Haledjian onto the front porch. "It got so no store in town would send anything on a telephone order. Had to have it in writing. Aside from a daily milk and newspaper delivery, the only visitors who climbed up her regularly were the weekly grocery boy and Doc Bentley, both due tomorrow. You can see why."

Haledjian gazed down a long slope of underbrush to the road below. The driveway to the house was overgrown and impassable, and deliveries obviously had to be made on foot.

The famed sleuth sat down in a rocking chair, the only object on the sagging porch beside two unopened newspapers.

"Who was the last person to see Mrs. Treddor alive?"

"Mrs. Carson, probably," said the sheriff. "Early on the day of Mrs. Treddor's death, she was driving by and noticed the old lady come out on the porch to take in her bottle of milk."

The sheriff paused. "Mrs. Treddor was supposed to have fifty thousand dollars hidden some place. We can't find it, or any clues."

"Except for that anonymous telephone call," corrected Haledjian. "The murderer never figured you wouldn't investigate within the hour!"

Whom did Haledjian suspect?

The milkman, who thought he didn't have to make his daily delivery. There were two newspapers on the porch, but no bottles of milk.

The Case of the
LOCKED ROOM

"I think I've been taken for ten thousand dollars, but I can't figure out how it was done," said Archer Skeat, the blind violinist, to Dr. Haledjian, as the two friends sat in the musician's library.

"Last night Marty Scopes dropped by," continued Skeat. "Marty had a ginger ale — and we got to chatting about the locked room mysteries till I made this crazy ten-thousand-dollar bet.

"Marty then went to the bar over there, filled a glass with six cubes of ice and gave it to me. He took a bottle of ginger ale and left the room.

"I locked the door and the windows from the inside, felt to make sure that Marty's glass held only ice, and put it into the wall safe behind you. Then I turned off the lights and sat down to wait.

"The bet was that within an hour Marty could enter the dark, locked room, open the locked safe, take out the glass, remove the ice, pour in half a glass of ginger ale, lock the safe, and leave the room, locking it behind him — all without my hearing him!

"When the alarm rang after an hour, I had heard nothing. Confidently, I unlocked the door. I kept Marty whistling in the hall when I crossed the room to the opposite wall and opened the safe. The glass was inside. By heavens, it was half filled with ginger ale and only ginger ale. I tasted it! How did he do it?"

"Undoubtedly by means of an insulated bag," replied Haledjian after a moment's thought. "There is nothing wrong with your hearing. But no man could have heard —"

Heard what?

Ice melting. Marty had brought him frozen cubes of ginger ale. After setting up the bet, he had slipped the ginger ale cubes into the glass. While they melted in the glass inside the safe, Marty waited in the hall!

The Case of the
LOOKOUT

Dr. Haledjian was the only customer in the little drugstore when the shooting started.

He had just taken his first sip of black coffee when three men dashed from the bank across the street, guns blazing.

As the holdup men jumped into a waiting car, a nun and a chauffeur sought refuge in the drugstore.

"You're both upset," said Haledjian. "Let me buy you a cup of coffee."

They thanked him. The nun ordered black coffee, the chauffeur a glass of root beer.

The three fell to talking about the flying bullets and had barely touched their drinks when sirens sounded.

The robbers had been captured and were being returned to the bank for identification.

Haledjian moved to a front window to watch.

As he returned to the counter, the nun and chauffeur thanked him again and departed.

The counterman had cleared the glass and cups. "Sorry, mister," he said to Haledjian. "I didn't know you weren't done."

The counterman looked at the two coffee cups he had just removed from the counter, and passing Haledjian the one without lipstick, said, "What do you think a chauffeur was doing around here? There isn't a limousine on the street."

Haledjian thought a moment. "Good grief!" he cried. "We had the gang's lookout right here!"

And he dashed out to make the capture.

What aroused Haledjian's suspicion?

The woman dressed as a nun admitted being the lookout after Haledjian had seized her down the block.

Haledjian had noticed the lipstick on her coffee cup too, and knew she was not a real nun, since nuns don't wear lipstick.

The Case of the
LOST CITY

"I'm really onto something big this time," said Bertie Tilford, the irrepressible Englishman with more get-rich-quick schemes than horsehair in a mattress factory.

He fished a letter from his pocket and pressed it to Dr. Haledjian. "Run your eyes on this, old boy!"

The letter, addressed to Bertie, was signed "Baron Stramm." Haledjian read:

"Am positive I have located the lost city of Heliopaulis which was buried by the eruption of Mount Vitras in 147 A.D. Can you rush me thirty thousand dollars to begin excavations?"

"Baron Stramm," explained Bertie, "came to see me before departing on his search for Heliopaulis last year. He said if he ever found the city, he'd let me in on the ground floor, so to speak. A half share of everything — if I backed him."

Bertie grinned smugly. "Can you imagine what a discovery like Heliopaulis will be worth?"

"Of course," said Haledjian. "You'd like to raise some of the thirty thousand from me?"

"A pittance, my dear chap. A mere bagatelle," said Bertie. "I'm doing you a favor. Let me have ten thousand and I'll make your fortune!"

"I don't know anything about your Baron Stramm," said Haledjian. "Or the lost city of Heliopaulis. But the man who wrote that letter is obviously not an archeologist. So no money today for your swindler, my boy!"

Why not?

A bona fide archeologist would never have written "in 147 A.D." A.D. means "in the year of the Lord," and unlike B.C. always precedes the date; as, A.D. 147.

The Case of the
MAESTRO'S
CHOICE

Even by the night of the concert, Gregory Pitz, the famous conductor, hadn't decided which of his star pupils, Ivan Poser or Mark Donn, would make his violin debut.

The anxious youths dressed in separate private dressing rooms. Fifteen minutes before curtain time, Pitz made up his mind.

He told Poser he had been selected; then he broke the sad news to Donn.

Ten minutes later Pitz went to fetch Poser for the performance. The youth lay dead in the middle of the tiny dressing room floor, shot through the head.

Trembling, Pitz locked the door and summoned his old friend, Dr. Haledjian, from the wings.

Haledjian urged the maestro to play the concert and followed him into Donn's dressing room.

Hearing that he was to perform after all — with-

89

out hearing why—Donn looked surprised and pleased. He straightened his tie, picked up his violin and bow, and followed Pitz downstairs and onto the stage.

The two musicians bowed to the applause. Donn waited stiffly till Pitz signaled the orchestra. Then the youth raised his violin to his chin.

A moment later Donn was stroking the opening notes. Haledjian telephoned the police and advised them to arrest the young violinist.

Why?

The fact that Donn was prepared to perform and therefore was aware of Poser's death indicated he was involved in the murder.

Had he been unaware, he would have stopped to rosin his bow and tune his violin before playing.

The Case of the
MISSING BUTTON

Matty Linden, a husky tenth-grade student, scowled at Inspector Winters. "You must be some kind of nut. I didn't slug Miss Casey, and I didn't steal her purse!"

"No? Unfortunately for you, a ninth-grade girl happened to enter the corridor where Miss Casey lay. The girl saw a boy in a dark cardigan sweater and brown pants leaving by the door at the far end."

The inspector paused and then demanded, "Do you always wear your sweater buttoned?"

"Sure," replied Matty. "Why?"

"Because you might have noticed the third button from the top is missing," snapped the inspector. He held up the missing button. "The girl who spotted you found the button clasped in Miss Casey's hand."

"I lost that button two days ago," retorted

Matty. "This girl — how could she be sure it was me in that long corridor?"

"She isn't positive — she saw only your back. But this missing button proves you did it. Lucky Miss Casey isn't badly hurt. Now, where's her purse?"

"Matty kept insisting he didn't know a thing about the slugging and theft," the inspector told Dr. Haledjian later.

"No doubt," said Haledjian, "the boy had some silly alibi about where he was when Miss Casey was slugged and robbed?"

"Right. He claims he got a note to be in the school boiler room at ten — fifteen minutes before Miss Casey was assaulted. He waited half an hour, but nobody showed up."

"I trust you made an arrest?" asked Haledjian.
What was the guilty student's error?

In trying to frame Matty Linden, the ninth-grade girl made too much of a point of the cardigan, which he always wore buttoned. Since she saw only the back of a boy leaving the corridor, she could not have known whether his sweater was a pullover or a cardigan unless she knew beforehand, having stolen the button from it.

The Case of
MOLLY'S MULE

Cyril Makin, the amateur amorist, sagged dejectedly into a chair in Dr. Haledjian's home. "I got slapped last night," he moaned. "I can't figure what was wrong with my pitch this time.

"I was trying to impress Libby McMurdoch," continued Cyril. "You know her — her father owns Greenpoint Farms, the big racing stable.

"Animals come before anything in the McMurdoch book. Why last year her old man scratched his ace thoroughbred from the Garden Classic because he suspected a sore hoof. Gave up a crack at a hundred thousand dollars!

"Well, I had to top that animal-before-money bit," Cyril continued. "So I unbottled my great-uncle, Death Valley Tim, and his faithful mule Molly M. I told Libby about how Uncle Tim and Molly M went into the desert in '89. That trip Uncle Tim hit the mother lode, richest gold strike

93

ever. But did he haul it right away? No, sir! Molly M was ailing, and Molly M came before anything.

"Uncle Tim just waited, week after week. Finally Molly M had her little one, Strike-It-Rich, but Uncle Tim waited another week till Molly M was strong enough to tote a load of gold.

"When Tim returned to the desert, he discovered a storm had wiped out all trace of the diggings. He never found the spot again. Five or six millions were lost by waiting for Molly M instead of making two or three quick trips, though the poor beast wasn't fit for heavy work."

"About there," broke in Haledjian, "Miss Libby McMurdoch, the animal-lover, decided that you weren't fit for her!"

Why not?

No mule — not even Molly M — can reproduce.

The Case of
MURDER AT
THE ZOO

The headlights of Dr. Haledjian's car flooded over a blond man darting across the road. Haledjian spun the steering wheel and slammed on the brakes. "Are you all right?" he called anxiously.

"I'm okay," the man gasped. "But there's somebody—I think he's dead—lying in the zoo. I was running to get the police."

Explaining he was a doctor, Haledjian persuaded the blond man to show him the "corpse." About a hundred yards from the road, near the giraffe enclosure, lay a figure in a doorman's uniform.

"He's just been slain," said Haledjian. "Shot in the back. Do you know him?"

"No," the man said. "My name is Chris Taylor. I was out for a walk when a car passed me a few minutes ago. It was traveling very slowly.

"The next thing I knew, an orange flame appeared in the back of the car. Then a giraffe began to scream as if in pain. The enclosure is visible from the road, and I saw one giraffe running in circles and suddenly collapse. I went to investigate and stumbled on the body here."

"I want to see the giraffe," muttered Haledjian. He climbed the fence and knelt beside the stricken animal. "Poor creature has been shot in the neck."

"The way I figure it," said Taylor, "the killer must have missed his man and hit the giraffe with his first shot. The second bullet found the mark, though."

"Undoubtedly that is what happened," agreed Haledjian. "Only for one thing. You weren't running to get help. You were running away!"

How did Haledjian know?

Taylor claimed that he stumbled on the dead man after being attracted by the "scream" of the giraffe. Unfortunately for his story, a giraffe is voiceless.

The Case of
MURDER
BEFORE THE
CONCERT

The body of pretty Frieda Dillon lay beside her green sedan in the driveway of the boarding house where she lived. She had been slain at 8 P.M., some fifteen minutes before she was due at the Civic Auditorium to perform in a concert slated for 8:30 P.M.

She had been shot twice. The first bullet had pierced her right thigh, leaving a large blood stain on her dark sheath skirt. The second and fatal bullet had pierced her heart, leaving a blood stain on her white blouse.

Inside the sedan was Miss Dillon's cello.

The police took testimony from three persons.

The landlady, Mrs. Wilson, who found the body, said Frieda had decided to attend the concert but not to play, because she had been annoyed by an over-ardent suitor, Bill Sanders, a fellow orchestra member. Frieda hadn't practiced her cello or taken it from the car in a week.

Bill Sanders insisted that he and Frieda had patched up their romance. She had told him she would play, and that she'd pick him up at 8:10 P.M. and they would drive together to the auditorium as they always did. But he had waited for her in vain.

Lazlo St. John, the conductor, said that the women members of the orchestra wore dark skirts and white blouses, and the men wore white jackets and black trousers, though minor details of style were optional. The orchestra members dressed at home. He added that Frieda undoubtedly could perform well without any practice, since the concert was a repeat program.

After reading the three statements, Haledjian immediately knew Sanders was lying.

How?

Haledjian knew that Frieda Dillon had no intention of playing with the orchestra, as Bill Sanders claimed. She was a cellist, and could not possibly have performed wearing a sheath skirt.

The Case of the
MURDERED CAMPER

Dr. Haledjian and Sheriff Monahan had scarcely finished supper when Wyatt Fulton burst into their camp clearing.

"Hurry, Sheriff," he cried. "Bob's been killed!"

During the five-minute tramp to his campsite, Fulton recounted what had happened.

"An hour ago, just as Bob and I were going to have coffee, two men with rifles stepped out of the woods. We mistook them for hunters till they announced a holdup.

"Bob jumped one, but the other struck him on the head with a rock. They tied us up and stole our money.

"I finally worked free and cut Bob loose — he was dead. I remembered you'd gone camping, Sheriff. So I looked for your fire."

At Fulton's campsite, Haledjian's practiced eye missed nothing.

Bob Swamm's body lay on its back near the fire. Near the body were several strands of rope and a bloody rock. A yard away was the uncut rope that had apparently been used to bind Fulton.

Two sleeping bags and two knapsacks lay on the ground. On a large flat stone were pairs of plates, forks, cups, and knives. The cups were unused.

"Bob Swamm died about an hour ago, probably from the blow on the head," Haledjian said.

For a moment afterward the only sound in the clearing was the hissing from the fire as the small black coffee pot cast boiling drops over the brim and onto the flaming logs below.

Haledjian broke the silence. "A neatly staged murder scene, Fulton. But you made one fatal mistake."

What was the mistake?

Had the coffee pot been put on the fire before the two holdup men murdered Swamm, "an hour ago," as Fulton claimed, the water would have boiled away far below the brim of the small pot. Hence Fulton had just put on the pot before running to fetch the sheriff.

The Case of the
MURDERED SKIER

When a mid-January thaw melted the snow drifts in the Adirondack Mountains, a late-model sports car was found parked on a side road near the Guilden Ski Lodge. Inside were the bodies of May Elliot and Roger Kirk, victims of rifle shots. Both had registered at the resort a week earlier under fictitious names.

"We checked out Miss Elliot — nothing," said Inspector Winters to Dr. Haledjian as the two men stood in the trophy-hung living room of Roger Kirk.

Haledjian read a maple plaque awarded to Kirk as runner-up in the 1959 World Water Ski championships.

Then he moved to a table whereon were four birthday gifts, opened by the police. Haledjian studied a book on underwater treasure hunting from Abe Merkin; a pair of ski poles from Curt

Gowan; a spear-gun from Jim Shick; and a monogramed pith helmet from Walt Parker.

"Kirk's been living off his reputation for years," said the inspector. "He taught water skiing and skin diving to celebrities. Maybe if he'd stuck to his line he'd still be alive.

"He was a schemer. Never told anybody what he was up to, certainly not about the rendezvous with May Elliot. He invited four men to his birthday party here; they showed up, but he didn't, because that night he registered at the ski lodge under a phony name.

"I spoke with the four men," went on the inspector. "Kirk wrote them the same invitation: 'Before I go off skiing, come over and wish me a happy birthday. Tuesday. My place. 8:00 P.M.' The guests—Merken, Gowan, Shick, and Parker—left their gifts with the building superintendent and went home. They all claim they didn't know where he was going skiing."

"One of them is obviously lying," said Haledjian. *Which one?*

Curt Gowan, whose gift of ski poles showed he knew Kirk, the water-ski ace, was going to ski on snow when he should have assumed, as the others did, that he was going south to ski on water.

The Case of the
MURDERED WIFE

Dr. Haledjian finished examining the body of Maureen Page which lay on the maroon carpet of her fashionable Gables home.

"Mrs. Page was struck fatally on the head with the butt of that pistol," the famous sleuth said. "She probably was hit four or five times."

The .38 had been found near the body. Sheriff Monahan was carefully dusting it for fingerprints.

"I've telephoned her husband at his office," the sheriff said. "I only told him he'd better hurry home. Hate the job of breaking the news of her murder. Will you do it?"

"All right," Haledjian agreed heavily watching the body being carried to an ambulance. Then he sat down to wait for John Page.

The ambulance had driven off when the distraught husband burst through the front door. "What happened? Where's Maureen?"

"I'm sorry to have to tell you this. She was murdered about two hours ago," said Haledjian. "Your cook found the body in the living room and telephoned the sheriff."

"I can't find fingerprints on the murder gun," interrupted the sheriff, holding the weapon wrapped in a handkerchief. "I'll have the lab go over it thoroughly."

Page's facial muscles twitched with emotion as he stared at the outline of the gun through the handkerchief. Suddenly he gripped the sheriff's arm. "Find the fiend who clubbed Maureen to death. I'll put up a fifty-thousand-dollar reward!"

"Save your money," said Haledjian. "The murderer won't be that hard to find!"

Why not?

Had John Page been innocent, he would not have known that his wife had been "clubbed" to death. Seeing the murder gun, he should have assumed she had been shot.

The Case of the
MURDERING RIVAL

"Molly Fipps was murdered in the basement of her apartment house yesterday," Inspector Winters told Dr. Haledjian.

"The murder weapon, a bread knife, was wiped clean of fingerprints. But we have two suspects, Dereck Comin and Eric Hoder, a pair of rival suitors."

The inspector related the details of the case.

"Molly's body, dressed in sneakers, shorts, and a white sweatshirt, was found by the janitor at noon, about an hour after the time of death. She had been duly registered as a crewman aboard Derek Comin's yacht for the ocean powerboat race that afternoon. She'd been in his crew before.

"Comin got to the docks around noon, an hour late. He claims he was delayed by motor trouble, which he fixed himself. Nobody saw him do it. He could have spent the hour killing Molly.

"Eric Hoder was seen talking to Molly that morning in front of her apartment. He claims he asked her to lunch. He says she refused because she had an afternoon engagement and had to hurry to the hairdresser.

"Hoder, an artist, says he then went back to his studio and painted all day. But he has no confirming witnesses either.

"I talked to Comin and Hoder for hours," concluded the sheriff. "I can't shake their stories. One of them is lying, I'm sure of it."

"So am I," said Haledjian.

Whom did Haledjian suspect?

Haledjian knew Hoder lied in saying Molly told him earlier she was going to the hairdresser. No woman who was going yachting would have her hair set!

The Case of the
MUSICAL THIEF

The visiting British Army Band, under the baton of Sir Roger Lindsey-Haven, had just struck up "God Save the Queen" when two gun shots rang out.

Dr. Haledjian and Inspector Winters remained in their places until the anthem ended. Then they raced up the aisle and into the streets of New York City.

Two blocks away they found three policemen subduing a stocky man in a blue suit. One of the policemen reported to the inspector:

"The concert hall box office was held up a few minutes ago by a thickset masked man in a blue suit. He put six thousand dollars and his gun into a paper bag and fled.

"We spotted this fellow walking too quickly. When we ordered him to halt and he didn't, we shot into the air. He broke into a run and hurled a paper bag down the sewer."

"You're crazy!" screamed the prisoner. "I haven't been past the concert hall! I heard a band playing 'God Save the Queen,' and somebody shouted, 'Halt or I'll shoot.'

"I haven't done anything," he insisted. "I figured the police were after somebody else. I heard shots so I ran to get off the street. I tossed a bag of orange peels into the sewer, not money! I got excited."

Just then the concert resumed. Despite the intervening buildings, strains of a march could be heard distinctly.

"You have a good ear for music," commented Haledjian. "And good eyes. There's a poster over the box office announcing tonight's performance of the British Army Band. You'd have done better not to have read it!"

What did Haledjian mean?

The prisoner insisted he had not been near the concert hall. Yet he never would have called the anthem he heard "God Save the Queen" unless he had seen the poster and knew a British band was performing.

Had he been innocent, he would have named the music by its American words, "My Country, 'Tis of Thee."

The Case of
NEWTON
THE KNIFE

As the headwaiter seated Dr. Haledjian and Octavia in a secluded corner, the sleuth observed a diner at the next table catch a squirt of grapefruit in his left ear.

"Puts me in mind of the case of Newton the Knife. Care to hear about it?" said Haledjian.

"Couldn't we order first?" asked Octavia.

"Newton the Knife," began Haledjian, hardly noticing the interruption, "was a notorious cutthroat. His body was found in a dingy Brooklyn bar. A bullet had entered his left ear and lodged midway in his brain, causing death instantly.

"The bullet matched the gun of Figaro Jones, another hoodlum and Newton's sworn enemy.

"Figaro said he was the last customer in the bar at closing time when Newton entered, raised his famous knife above his head, and, cursing in Russian, ran at him.

109

"Figaro claimed he shot in self-defense as Newton charged him head-on, like a maddened bull. Newton's knife was found clutched in his right hand. He apparently fell holding it as he died.

"Figaro's self-defense plea was seconded by the bartender, the only eye witness. But even without the bartender's phony corroboration, I knew Figaro's account was pure fabrication," concluded Haledjian. "Can you think why?"

"I'm too hungry to think," said Octavia. "Why? *Why?*"

It would have been impossible for Figaro to shoot Newton through the ear while Newton was charging him "head-on."

The Case of the
OFFICE
SHOOTING

As Inspector Winters looked around the cubbyhole office of John Stahl, Bart Rea said, "I touched nothing—except the desk telephone. I called you right away."

John Stahl's body lay on the threadbare carpet behind his desk. Near his right hand was a large French pistol.

"Tell me what happened," snapped the inspector.

"John asked me to come here," began Rea. "Then right off he started raving about his wife and me.

"I told him he was way out. But John has a red-flag temper. I couldn't calm him down. He doesn't know what he's doing when he goes crazy mad.

"Suddenly he jumped up and shouted, 'I'm going to kill you!' With practically one motion he yanked open the top drawer of his desk and took out a gun and fired at me. He missed. I shot back immediately. It was self-defense."

The inspector inserted a pencil into the barrel of the big French pistol and lifted it from beside the corpse. Opening the top desk drawer, he thoughtfully slid the gun inside.

"Rea's a private investigator," the inspector told Dr. Haledjian that night. "His pistol is registered to him. It fired the death bullet."

"We found a bullet from the French pistol in the wall opposite the desk — the shot Rea says Stahl fired first. The pistol bears Stahl's fingerprints, but he didn't have a license for it, and we can't trace it."

"You charged Rea with murder, I hope?" said Haledjian.

"What else could I do? He's already confessed."

What was Rea's slip?

Rea claimed that he had "touched nothing," and that Stahl "with practically one motion" had opened the drawer, taken out the gun, and fired. Even a less hot-tempered man would have never bothered to close the drawer after pulling out a gun with intent to kill. The inspector found the drawer closed, remember?

The Case of the
OPEN DOOR

Working calmly and efficiently, Greg Verner hanged Brendon Trom in the attic of Trom's rented house. It was not until Verner tried to shut the front door that he hit a snag. The lock was jammed.

"Better get out of here," he thought, casting anxious glances at the dense woods surrounding the house.

Two hours later he was driving back to the house with Dr. Haledjian.

"Brendon's been morose since his divorce. I should have visited him, but nobody knew where he was hiding out. I got his address this afternoon when he telephoned me to say he was contemplating suicide. I thought you'd better come with me and perhaps have a talk with him.

"He said it was a white stucco house, 621 Delaware Avenue, over the phone," went on Verner. "Here we are."

Haledjian left the car first. Finding the front door ajar, he entered and switched on the lights. Five minutes later the two men found Brendon Trom in the attic.

As they stood silently staring at the body, a door chime sounded downstairs.

With Haledjian right behind him, Verner hastened to the back door. There stood a teen-age girl. "Mother asked me to return this bottle of milk to Mr. Trom," she said.

Haledjian took the milk and after she had gone he called the police.

"You better arrest Mr. Verner on suspicion of murder," he said when they arrived.

Why?

Although Verner carefully built up the impression he had never visited the Trom house before, he knew while standing in the attic that the chime was from the back door.

The Case of the

ORANGE BIRD

For years Mrs. Sydney, the wealthiest dowager in New York City, had vainly tried to outwit Dr. Halediian. As the famous criminologist selected a cigar from the tray held by the Sydney butler, a wicked gleam came into his hostess's eye. It was time for playing stump-the-detective. . . .

"John DeMott, Paul Houk, and Lee Roach were partners in a successful New York jewelry business," began Mrs. Sydney. "Last January they flew down to the Florida Keys to spend a month at De-Mott's lodge.

"One afternoon DeMott took Houk, an avid fisherman but a non-swimmer, out on his forty-foot cruiser. Roach, whose hobby was bird-watching, remained behind.

"Roach says he was sitting behind the lodge when he spied an exotic orange bird, a species new to him, fly by. He followed it to the front of the house, and through binoculars watched it building a nest, high in a palm tree.

"Quite by chance, he moved the binoculars out to the water and saw DeMott and Houk struggling on the yacht. Roach says DeMott shoved Houk overboard and held his head under water.

"DeMott claimed that Houk had leaned over the side to gaff a fish, and, losing his balance, fell into the ocean. He drowned before DeMott could reach him.

"The coroner ascribed death to drowning. At the trial, it was simply DeMott's word against Roach's.

"The jury deliberated less than five minutes," concluded Mrs. Sydney. "No doubt, my dear doctor, you won't need so long to realize who was lying."

Haledjian didn't. Do you?

Although an experienced bird-watcher, Roach didn't know his tropical flora. Obviously, he didn't watch a bird building a nest in a palm tree as he claimed. Palm trees don't have branches, only long slippery fronds; and birds can't perch — much less nest — on them.

The Case of the
OVERHEARD KILLER

Steve Corrigan, the mad-dog killer, was shot to death in a Detroit boarding house during a gun battle with police, who acted on an anonymous telephone tip.

Two days earlier a man had held up a Toledo bank and had slain two cashiers. A guard spotted a scar on the masked gunman's right hand. Within an hour the police had the tell-tale description booming over the loudspeakers of every transportation center within a fifty-mile radius of the crime.

Everyone with an eye to collecting the well-publicized fifty-thousand-dollar reward began insisting he was the anonymous tipster. The Detroit police asked Dr. Haledjian to screen the claimants.

The first was Bill Kempton, who told his story confidently.

"Just as my brother Carl boarded the bus to Bowling Green, the description came over the bus depot's loudspeaker. Carl got a seat in the back, and as the bus started, he noticed a man with a scar on his right hand sitting midway up the bus.

"The man leaned over and said to the red-headed woman across the aisle, 'I better get off at the first stop and head for Detroit.'

"Carl's a deaf-mute and can read lips. He saw the scarred man pass the woman a note and say, 'Meet me in two days at this address.'

"Carl had me telephone the police anonymously when he got home. He had seen the red-haired woman crumple the note after reading it and drop it on the floor. Carl was the last off the bus and he picked it up. Here it is."

"It's the address of the boarding house where the killer was shot by the police, all right," said Haledjian. "Just as the newspapers gave it. Bring the next tipster, sergeant!"

What was wrong with Kempton's story?

The note was an obvious fake. Carl, the "deaf-mute," might be able to read lips and so know what the scarred man said. But Carl never could have attached importance to his remarks unless he had heard Corrigan's description broadcast over the depot loudspeakers as he boarded the bus.

The Case of the
PARKED CAR

The sleek foreign convertible was like many others in the Midcity garage except for the dead man's brown shoes and socks protruding from the opened driver's door.

"He was J. William Clancy, New York's top expert on men's fashions," Inspector Winters told Dr. Haledjian. "I sent for you because something is odd about this case.

"Here's what we've got," continued the inspector. "Clancy had a date for 8 P.M. with Denise Mills, a model, two nights ago. When he didn't show up, she telephoned his roommate, Kurt Wagner. Wagner checked on Clancy's movements.

"Wagner turned up nothing and called us. After backchecking, we found Clancy's body. It looks like Clancy was about to take out his car for the date with Miss Mills when another car hit him and kept going. Clancy dragged himself to the telephone in his car, but died before he could use it."

Haledjian bent over the body. He carefully studied the blood which had flowed from a corner of the dead man's mouth and dried upon his striped shirt and brown suitcoat lapel.

"Notice his watch," said the inspector. "It's smashed — the hands stopped at 7:45. The medical examiner says he died about forty-eight hours ago. That ties in — forty-eight hours ago Clancy was headed for his 8 P.M. date with Miss Mills."

"Quite wrong, inspector," said Haledjian. "The smashed watch is an inept attempt to misrepresent the time of death. Unquestionably Clancy died at least two hours earlier."

Haledjian straightened and stepped from the body. "The clumsy cover-up indicates Clancy was murdered!"

How did Haledjian know?

Only a man ignorant of fashion would have worn brown shoes, brown suit, and a striped shirt for a date at 8 P.M. After dark, Clancy, the fashion expert, would have worn black shoes, white shirt, and a dark suit.

The Case of the

PAYROLL TRUCK

Driving through deserted farm country a few miles from Fort Olmstead, Dr. Haledjian suddenly came upon an army truck that had crashed into a tree beside the road.

As he stopped his car, a jeep came from the opposite direction carrying two officers and two sergeants, all wearing side arms. A sergeant leaped out of the jeep and ran to the truck.

"They've been shot, major!" he shouted.

"I'm a doctor," said Haledjian. He opened the cab door. The driver was dead; the soldier beside him was dying.

"I can't do anything for them," murmured Haledjian to the major who had hurried over. The famous sleuth saw the cross on the officer's collar. "This is your work now, chaplain."

The major nodded and moved to the dying man.

The other officer, a captain, said to Haledjian,

"That's the fort's payroll truck. The way I see it, those poor boys were ambushed, but the driver managed to keep going till he died.

"Sergeant," the captain called. "Get the money out of the truck and put it in the jeep."

When the money had been transferred, the captain said, "Chaplain, you better stay here. We'll get help back to you as fast as we can. And don't trust anybody, you hear?"

The captain and the two sergeants sped off in the jeep. Haledjian waited only until they were around a bend to flatten the chaplain with a straight right to the jaw.

Why?

Haledjian realized the chaplain would shoot him and take off in his car the moment he saw his chance. The four soldiers were obviously impostors, as all were "wearing side arms," including the chaplain. But service chaplains are forbidden to carry weapons.

The Case of the
PHANTOM
KILLER

"This one gives me the shudders," admitted Sheriff Monahan. "The killer operated on a split-second timetable, yet he apparently picked his victim at random.

"Brentwood Hills is just a two-minute stop on the express run to Kansas City," continued the sheriff. "The killer got off the train and walked into the two-room station. Tim Doherty was inside his office with Reverend Archibald. The office is separated from the outer room, or waiting room, by a swinging door set two feet off the ground. The two men were standing close to it, reading a church pamphlet.

"From where he stood in the waiting room, the killer could see only the trouser cuffs and shoes of the two men, and both were wearing blue trousers and black shoes. Yet he put all three bullets on the right side of the door, where Doherty was.

"The minister didn't hear a report, which means that the killer either had a silencer or timed his shots with the screams of the locomotive whistle, or both. Doherty collapsed, and by the time Reverend Archibald had time to look, the train was pulling out. The killer had to be on it since there wasn't anybody in sight.

"We checked with the railroad people. Nobody bought a ticket to Brentwood Hills. Nobody, as far as we could determine, got off or on there.

"So it comes up this way," concluded the sheriff heavily. "A psycho picks a small town, slips off the train unnoticed, kills someone he never sees, and somehow slips aboard again. We'll never get him in a million years."

"Quite wrong, inspector," disagreed Haledjian. "After all, we don't have more than a dozen or so suspects to sift through."

What did Haledjian mean?

Haledjian knew that the killer in two minutes had to be able to: get on and off a train without attracting notice, know the duration of train whistles, and, most revealing of all, identify his victim merely by glancing at his shoes.
He was, therefore, a Pullman porter.

The Case of the
PHONY
FINANCIER

"Last week I pulled off my best act yet," groaned Cyril Makin, the backfiring ladykiller. "I can't figure out how Ginger Faulk knew I was bluffing."

Makin flopped despondently into an armchair in Dr. Haledjian's study and recounted his latest tale of curdled courtship.

"Ginger's father is head of Affiliated Banks of California. She's accustomed to million-dollar deals being closed on the telephone.

"I decided to trump anything she'd ever heard on Mr. Bell's business line. So I had her meet me at noon for lunch in Behlen's, the swankiest restaurant in Los Angeles.

"After we had ordered, I called for a table phone. I asked to talk with Northern Airlines at Kennedy Airport, New York.

"John Gotch, an old buddy, was at the other

end of the line, speaking from Behlen's kitchen. 'Page Mr. Leonard Coffin,' I said. 'It's urgent!'

"After three minutes, John came on again as Coffin.

" 'We got the Western award,' I said. 'Tell Gristoffolis in Zurich the deal — reoffer the bonds at 99½ per cent for the fifteen-year maturity. The selling commission of 1 per cent on the long bonds and ½ per cent on the short ought to net three million.' Then I hung up.

" 'Coffin,' I explained to Ginger, 'is taking the 1 P.M. flight to Zurich. By suppertime I should have the European cartel's answer.' "

"You were lucky," commented Haledjian. "Miss Faulk didn't throw something at you."

What was Makin's slip?

Because of the three-hour difference in time between the coasts, Makin's call, made in Los Angeles around noon, would have missed Coffin, flying at 1 P.M. from New York, by two hours.

The Case of the
POST OFFICE BOX

"Don't tell me Joey de Santos just handed over the Pondfield necklace to you!" bellowed Inspector Winters.

Nick the Nose backed against the wall of the inspector's office. "Now wait," he begged. "It wasn't like that. See this key? It's to Joey's mailbox in the Maple Street post office."

The greasy little informer shifted his feet nervously.

"You been looking for the Pondfield necklace, ain't you?" he asked. "Old man Pondfield insured it for a million. I bet the insurance company is breathing down your neck."

"The insurance people want the police to recover the necklace," admitted the inspector. "What are you selling?"

"The necklace," said Nick grandly. "Before the

cops shot him onto a slab, Joey mailed the necklace to his postal box—"

"Nuts!" exclaimed the inspector. "Are you telling me Joey just made you a present of his mailbox key?"

"No," said Nick quickly. "Last month when he was hiding after the Rockland job, he sent me out to a hardware store to have his car keys duplicated. Gave me his whole key ring. I duplicated everything on it, and kept the extras for myself. Just in case.

"When Joey got riddled yesterday, and the necklace ain't anywhere, I begin to think. Sure enough, one of the keys I had made fits his mailbox. The necklace is in one of them insulated bags. Now I figure it's worth—"

Nick the Nose's voice halted in a gasp as the inspector lifted him by the seat of the pants. Dr. Haledjian, who was coming into the office, held the door wide for one of Nick's head-first departures.

Why did Nick the Nose get the heave-ho?

Nick the Nose struck out in stating he had the key to Joey's mailbox duplicated at a hardware store. No keysmith will duplicate a United States post office key.

The Case of the
PUZZLED
HAIRDRESSER

"I can't figure out who learned I was taking the week's receipts to the bank on Thursday, a day early," said Mr. John, the hairdresser. "Every week for the past eight years I've taken the money at noon on Friday."

"Stop worrying," said Dr. Haledjian, as he finished bandaging Mr. John's head. "You're lucky to be alive. Whoever waylaid you in the alley must have used a piece of lead pipe."

"What I don't understand is who knew I was going, and where," said Mr. John.

"Whom did you tell?"

"Only my wife, Clara. At two o'clock I told her I was going to the bank."

"Did anyone overhear you?"

"There were three customers in the shop — new ones. I didn't even speak with them. Clara took care of two of them, and my brother Ted did the other. I recall all three women were seated under hair dryers, watching me, when I spoke with Clara about going to the bank."

"Where was Ted?"

"Out on a coffee break," replied Mr. John. "It couldn't have been either Ted or Clara."

"If you're so positive," said Haledjian thoughtfully, "we have only one suspect."

"Who?"

"Why, the one who couldn't possibly have overheard you if you screamed at the top of your lungs," replied Haledjian.

Whom did Haledjian mean?

None of the three women sitting under the hair driers could have heard Mr. John tell his wife he was going to the bank; hair driers simply make too much noise.

Therefore, Haledjian knew it had to be the woman who was deaf — and who could read lips.

The Case of the
RACKETEER'S DEATH

"The life policy on Mugsy McGurk, the labor racketeer, has a no-murder clause," said Henderson, the insurance investigator.

"You mean that if it turns out someone killed him, your company won't have to pay a cent?" asked Dr. Haledjian.

"Correct," acknowledged Henderson. "That's why I need your help. I can only suspect murder. Here are the few facts I have.

"McGurk died on the train to Miami. He had imbibed heavily in the club car until midnight. Then, helped by a waiter, he staggered to his berth, a lower in car 1056, and lay down without undressing. In a drunken stupor, he accidentally asphyxiated himself by burying his head in the pillow—or so it would seem.

"When he was found in the morning," continued Henderson, "his mouth and nose were clear of the pillow. It is thought he rolled when the train made a jolting halt about 1 A.M.

"A conductor had stopped the train—pulled the emergency cord—because he saw a man jumping off the last car. The man could have been McGurk's killer. Come into the next room, doctor. You'll see everything taken from McGurk's berth."

Haledjian viewed the articles piled on a square table. Besides the sheets, blankets, and a pillow belonging to the Pullman company, there was a mound of McGurk's clothes. Also the contents of his overnight bag. Among the latter were a pair of white pajamas, bedroom slippers, and a yellow bathrobe.

"Not much," conceded Henderson, "to prove murder."

"One article proves it," corrected Haledjian. *What was the article?*

Haledjian reasoned the killer had smothered McGurk with a pillow and then, fearing it held his fingerprints, took it with him. The article that gave the killing away was the pillow—the missing one. All train berths are made up with two.

The Case of the
RELUCTANT
WITNESS

Dr. Haledjian and Sheriff Monahan walked slowly down the path that stretched between James Ernst's newly painted rear porch and his tool shed in the back yard.

"From any place along this path," said Sheriff Monahan, "Ernst could have seen Fred Kolp being slain. He's our only possible witness, but he denies seeing anything."

"What do you make of these?" asked Haledjian, pointing to the drops of white paint that had fallen in a line along the path.

"Ernst," answered the sheriff, "had finished painting his porch and was bringing the paint can to the shed about the time the killing took place. Ernst claims he didn't realize the can had sprung a leak till he got into the tool shed."

Haledjian examined the paint drops more carefully.

133

From the porch to about midpoint along the path the paint had fallen in nearly circular drops every three feet. From midpoint to the tool shed, the drops were spaced about nine feet apart and were longer and narrower.

Haledjian was not surprised to find the padlock hanging from the inside latch of the tool shed.

"Ernst is absolutely terrified," said the sheriff. "He's clammed up tight. If he knows more than he's telling, I'll have to prove he saw Fred Kolp slain to make him talk."

"No doubt he fears the killer's vengeance if he admits having seen the murder," said Haledjian. "But he saw it, all right!"

How did Haledjian know?

The drops of paint told Haledjian that Ernst was midway along the path when he saw the killing. From that point to the tool shed — where the latch on the inside indicated he had locked himself in — the drops were spaced farther apart and were longer and narrower, showing he had suddenly broken into a run.

The Case of the
RESCUE AT SEA

"Thank heaven you saw me!" exclaimed Tom Bond as he feebly helped make fast his battered yawl to Dr. Haledjian's chartered fishing boat.

Haledjian reached over the side and assisted the bedraggled yachtsman aboard.

Bond staggered into the shade of the cabin and sagged upon a berth. He removed his cap to wipe the perspiration from his brow, revealing a bald, freckled head.

"Drink this," said Haledjian, holding out a cup of water.

Bond gulped it frantically, asked for a second, and when he had downed it, told of his ordeal.

"Ben Page and I were sailing for Bimini when the storm hit us. The sails, rudder, and radio went in the first five minutes. We barely managed to keep afloat.

"We drifted five days, lost. Three days ago our

fresh water supply gave out. Ben went crazy with the heat and thirst. He started to drink the ocean water. I tried to restrain him—I hit him. He—he struck his head against the starboard rail. He's dead! It's my fault!"

Haledjian climbed into Bond's disheveled yacht. In the little cabin he found Ben Page laid out on his back, dead. The criminologist studied the bruise on Page's jaw and the one at the base of his skull.

Back on the fishing boat, he warned Bond grimly, "You're going to have to tell the police a better tale than the one you told me!"

Why didn't Haledjian believe Bond?

Haledjian knew that Bond's story of hitting Page and accidentally killing him while restraining him from drinking ocean water was false. If the supply of fresh water had given out "three days ago," as Bond claimed, he would have been dehydrated, and therefore could not have wiped "the perspiration from his brow."

The Case of the
SEALED ROOM

On the evening of April 1 Dr. Haledjian was dining with Octavia when he saw a waiter slip on the glassy surface of the dance floor and land amid a welter of broken dishes, stuffed lobster, and very tossed salad.

"Puts me in mind of the famous sealed room case," said Haledjian. "Want to hear about it?"

"I'd rather dance," said Octavia. "But go ahead."

"H. Henderson Calborn III, the eccentric millionaire," began Haledjian, "had a windowless room in his mansion sealed off. In this impregnable repository he kept only one item — the greatest treasure of his entire fortune — the sarcophagus of Tutomkin IV, Pharaoh of Egypt.

"One night Calborn heard a noise within the room. It sounded like somebody was moving the sarcophagus! The next morning he had welders burn open the six-inch steel door.

"Lo, the sarcophagus was gone!

"Rushing into the room, Calborn slipped and fell flat on the floor. From this uncommon position he could closely observe another phenomenon. The entire floor had been freshly varnished!

"He called me immediately. Examining the room, I perceived the difficulty of anyone entering by the steel door and then vanishing with a four-ton sarcophagus. When I asked Calborn if he had any enemies, he named two — Klondike Kate and Indian Joe.

"Now," concluded Haledjian, "keeping in mind today is April Fool's Day, can you tell me how I deduced which was the thief?"

"Being a fool doesn't help me," sighed Octavia. "Which one?"

Can you guess?

Indian Joe, the "vanishing American." (Ugh!)

The Case of the
SHATTERED
DOOR

The 6-foot-4, 240-pound body of Earl Moon lay on the tile veranda amid a welter of shattered glass.

Dr. Haledjian studied the left side of Moon's jaw, which was bruised outside and bloody inside from a cut caused by two broken teeth. The bruise on the back of the head showed where Moon had struck the tiles. The back of the dead man's sports jacket was stitched with glass splinters.

"Apparently somebody punched Moon awfully hard on the side of the jaw," mused Haledjian. "Moon was thrown backward and he crashed through the closed sliding glass door. Falling, he struck his head on the veranda tiles and died of a broken neck."

"That confirms the account we have from Buster Epps, a neighbor," said Inspector Winters.

Epps moved from behind the inspector and

stared in disbelief at the body. He seemed still in a state of shock.

"I was tending my roses about half an hour ago when I noticed Moon and a stranger standing near this glass door. The stranger was not quite so tall as Moon, but just as broad. And he handled himself like a professional boxer.

"They seemed to be quarreling, but the door was shut and I couldn't overhear distinctly," continued Epps. "Suddenly Moon swung his fist. The stranger sidestepped expertly and hooked a left to Moon's jaw. Moon went crashing through the glass. He struck his head—I could hear the crack! The stranger fled immediately. I called the police when I couldn't overtake him."

"Now, now, Mr. Epps," said Haledjian. "Suppose you tell us what really happened."

Why didn't Haledjian believe Epps?

The stranger could not possibly have hit Moon on the left side of the jaw with a left hook. Had Moon exposed his left side, the natural blow would have been a right cross or a straight right.

140

The Case of the
STAMP
COLLECTOR

"I came in to help Mr. Dunning to bed," said Brock, the aged family servant. "I found him like this and summoned you from the living room immediately."

The 85-year-old John Dunning, a noted philatelist, lay slumped over his desk, dead of a blow which had been struck to the base of the skull within the past five minutes.

"When I entered, I thought I heard the rear door close," said Brock. "It leads to a back stairway."

Haledjian examined the five objects on the desk. There were a pair of tweezers, a stamp album, a stamp catalogue, and a bottle of benzine with an eyedropper for use in detecting water marks. A quartz floor lamp cast eerie ultraviolet rays over the dead man's left shoulder.

"Mr. Dunning had been appraising a stamp collection for a friend this evening," Brock explained.

Haledjian walked out of the room onto the balcony overlooking the living room, where the costume party, given by Dunning's granddaughter, was in sway.

"Who benefits from his will?"

"Why, I do," replied Brock. "And everyone at the party."

Haledjian studied the costumed merrymakers till his eye fell upon a young man dressed as Sherlock Holmes. His deer-stalker's cap tipped rakishly, he was examining the eyes of a pretty Salome through a large magnifying glass while blowing smoke from a meerschaum pipe.

"Call the police," Haledjian told Brock, "while I detain Mr. Holmes for questioning."

How come?

Haledjian realized the murder weapon was the one object missing from the stamp expert's desk — a magnifying glass.

The Case of the
STICKY BRUSH

"Thanks for the lift into town, Dr. Haledjian," said Joe May. "Mind stopping at Al Pohl's?"

"Not a bit," replied Haledjian, turning into a side road that led to Pohl's house of red brick with white wood porch, steps, and windows.

"I've been meaning to contact Al for two days," said May. "I need the wrench he borrowed last week."

Haledjian had barely brought the car to halt when May hopped out. "Won't be a second," he called, racing across the lawn and leaping over the steps. He skidded on the slate floor of the porch, but righted himself quickly.

Getting no answer to the doorbell, he walked to a window and rapped on a pane. "Al?" he shouted. "Al?"

Suddenly, jumping off the porch, he screamed, "Dr. Haledjian! Be—behind the shrubs!"

To the left of the porch behind a long row

of hibiscus set four feet from the brick wall, lay the body of Al Pohl. A six-foot stepladder had overturned on him. A can of white paint had spilled over his work shoes.

"Neck broken," said Haledjian. "About six hours ago."

The famous sleuth fingered the bristles of the paint brush near Al's right hand. "Sticky," he muttered.

Walking to the porch, he touched the white wood supports, the front door, the four steps, and the window sills. "Tacky," he said. "Al must have just finished painting them this morning when he met death."

The next day, after Joe May had been arrested, Haledjian told Sheriff Monahan:

"May thought that by pretending to discover the body with me he cleared himself of suspicion!"

What was May's error?

By saying, "I've been meaning to contact Al for two days," May expected to establish the fact that he hadn't been near the Pohl house during the killing.

Yet the fact that he twice jumped over the steps and knocked on the window pane rather than the door revealed that he knew the steps and door had been newly painted.

The Case of the
STOLEN RUBENS

Unable to sleep, Dr. Haledjian was walking about the grounds of his host, Percy Kilbrew, former right-handed pitching great, when he noticed a limousine by the back door.

Suddenly a man, fully clothed, stepped out the door and passed the driver what appeared to be a painting. Then the man dashed into the house and the car roared off, bowling over a garbage can with enough noise to awaken the dead.

In the 4 A.M. darkness Haledjian could not identify the men or the car. But the fate of the Rubens oil was plain enough—it was missing from the living-room wall.

Haledjian sprinted upstairs to his host's room and received a prompt, "Come in," to his knock. Kilbrew stood half-clothed by a rumpled bed, his right leg in his trousers and his left leg out.

"I heard the clatter and was just getting dressed to investigate," he said. "What happened?"

"The Rubens has been stolen," said Haledjian.

Kilbrew finished pulling on his trousers and followed Haledjian downstairs bare-footed.

In a few minutes Kilbrew's three other house guests descended the stairs.

John Ward, the art critic, wore an Oriental robe over black silk pajamas. Marty Latham, the singer, wore an old-fashioned nightshirt and cap. Everette Maloski, the painter, wore only tattered pajama bottoms.

"The Rubens is heavily insured," said Kilbrew. "But I don't care about the money. I want the painting back!"

"You don't have a worry on that score," Haledjian assured him.

Whom did Haledjian suspect?

Kilbrew — of wanting the insurance money and the painting. Although he claimed to be "just getting dressed," he was really getting undressed, since his left leg was out of his trousers. A right-handed man usually takes his right leg out first when undressing; he invariably puts his left leg in first when dressing.

The Case of the
SUICIDE ROOM

Sir Cecil Brookfield pulled back a massive door that opened off one of the arched corridors in his six-hundred-year-old castle in Wales.

Dr. Haledjian, a weekend guest, peered down into darkness.

"A room with four walls — and no floor," said Sir Cecil. "Or rather, a floor one hundred feet below the threshold.

"The room was designed to dispose in secret of troublesome vassals," explained Sir Cecil. "Later, when the beautiful wife of the first Lord Brookfield died in the plague, a grief-stricken young forester hurled himself to his doom here.

"A nasty legend developed from the forester's death," added Sir Cecil slowly. "It is that a young man will jump in the reign of every fourth baron. I am the fourth since the last suicide."

Sir Cecil shoved the heavy door shut. "I've ordered a mason from the village. He'll be here tomorrow to seal off the door."

Haledjian's bedroom was three doors from the "suicide room." As he was retiring for the night, he heard an eerie, dull thud. It could mean only one thing. He hastened to the corridor.

Sir Cecil was running toward the "suicide room." Together the two men swung open the massive door. Sir Cecil played a flashlight down into the dark pit.

The beam revealed the body of a young man.

"Ritchie, my wife's solicitor!" gasped Sir Cecil. "Why should he take his own life?"

"He didn't," corrected Haledjian. "He was pushed!"

How did Haledjian know?

The door to the "suicide room" was found closed. As the room had no floor, it would have been impossible for Ritchie to have closed the massive door from the inside and then turned and jumped.

The Case of the
TELLTALE CLOCK

Police found the body of Buffalo Fenn in his tenement room. He had been strangled by the electric cord of his alarm clock. Set for seven-thirty, the clock had stopped at seven.

Inspector Winters had Pete "The Hangman" Skones, Buffalo's inveterate foe, picked up for questioning.

The Hangman claimed that on the morning of Buffalo's murder, he had been in the middle of a three-day poker game with underworld friends. The friends swore he never left the hotel room.

A week passed without a new lead. Then Nick the Nose wheedled his way into the inspector's office.

The greasy little informer grinned. "I got something."

"It better be good," warned the inspector. "The last five times you got the boot."

"I got a witness to Buffalo's murder," announced Nick smugly. "Broadway Ben."

"Ben," said Nick, "had a room down the hall from Buffalo. He was passing Buffalo's room when he sees Buffalo's door ajar. He hears nothing at first but the ticking of Buffalo's alarm clock. And suddenly he don't hear even that.

"Then Ben hears a sound he don't like to hear at seven in the morning or any time else. He hides in a doorway at the end of the hall. Two minutes later he sees the Hangman scurry out of Buffalo's room and race downstairs.

"Ben is so scared after he reads what happened to Buffalo that he ain't looked at an alarm clock for a week. He's hiding, but I can take you to him for five grand. He'll testify."

"I don't pay for perjury," growled the inspector.

"He never improves," sighed Haledjian, entering the inspector's office and holding the door wide for Nick's flying exist.

Why was Nick booted?

Nick made too much of the ticking of the alarm clock, whose electric cord had been used to strangle Buffalo Fenn.

Alas for Nick, electric clocks don't tick.

The Case of the
UNUSED
SEAT BELT

When Inspector Winters slammed on the brakes, Dr. Haledjian would have been pitched through the windshield but for his seat belt.

The reason for the inspector's sudden stop was horribly evident.

A red sports car had come racing around the hairpin turn on the mountain road ahead. Out of control, the car had crashed through the guard rail.

The impact didn't stop the car, but it flung the driver straight up. He seemed to hang in the air a moment before plunging out of sight.

Haledjian and the inspector scrambled down the two hundred-foot precipice.

The driver's body was a shattered mass of broken bones and blood. About one hundred feet beyond, the sports car lay on its side, a total wreck.

"Strange," muttered the inspector, pointing to the seat belt, obviously unused, which lay in the fresh blood that covered the driver's bucket seat.

"I doubt that even a seat belt could have saved his life," said Haledjian.

"I better telephone the state police," said the inspector. "It looks like one more traffic fatality for the year. Do you think he fell asleep at the wheel?"

"No," said Haledjian. "He was murdered."

Why murder?

The fact that blood soaked the driver's seat though he had been cast free of the car when it hit the rail indicated he had bled before the accident: i.e., he had been killed and placed in the car, which had then been sent down the mountain road.

The Case of the
WAREHOUSE MURDER

"I heard a man scream twice," said Bob Lovell, an unemployed dog trainer. "Naturally, I stopped and looked through the ground floor window of the Universal Tire Company warehouse. I saw Mike Denton dragging a man toward a stack of white-wall tires, maybe ten or twelve feet high. I telephoned the cops right away."

"You didn't go inside the warehouse?" asked Inspector Winters.

"No. Why I wasn't ever near the building before," retorted Bob. "I was just out for a stroll. So what happens to a public-spirited citizen? He gets thrown in jail. Denton is your man, not me!"

The inspector nodded patiently. To the officer at the door he said, "Take Lovell back and bring in Mike Denton."

Denton, a laundry worker, admitted being inside the warehouse.

"I got an anonymous telephone call asking me to come there," he said. "The door was open, so I went in. I don't know nothing about a murder."

"Mel Capone's body, stabbed eight times, was found inside a twelve-foot-high stack of white-wall tires in the warehouse," said the inspector.

"The reason we found the body," continued the inspector, "was that the killer grew sloppy. He stacked the tires above Capone in a leaning column. The warehouse manager says he has his men pile the tires in perfect columns.

"I didn't kill Capone," blurted Denton. "I'm being framed!"

That night the inspector related the case to Dr. Haledjian.

"The warehouse workers," said the famous sleuth, "have picked out the killer for you, Inspector!"

What did Haledjian mean?

Lovell said he'd never been near the warehouse before. Yet he knew the tires toward which Capone was being dragged were white walls. From the window, he couldn't have seen anything but the treads, since the tires were stacked "ten or twelve feet high," by the warehouse workers in "perfect columns."

The Case of the
WHISPERING FINGER

A policeman patroling Midland Park heard the two shots, and racing toward the sounds, found the body of Willard Wilson sprawled on a little-used path near the boat basin. Wilson was dead of two bullet wounds in the head.

Sonny Dobein, an ex-convict seen in the park at the time of the murder, was held overnight by police, but released for lack of evidence. The dead man's widow immediately offered a fifty-thousand-dollar reward for the arrest of the killer.

The reward brought Nick the Nose, nostrils fluttering to the scent of fifty thousand dollars, into the office of Inspector Winters who was discussing the case with Dr. Haledjian.

"I got a witness says Sonny Dobein fingered Wilson," announced the greasy little informer.

"You always have a witness for a price," snapped

the inspector. "For fifty grand you ought to have a dozen!"

"This is on the level," insisted Nick. "Listen, my witness was in the park when Wilson was killed. He sees two men on a bench. One of them, Sonny Dobein, whispers to the other, 'Wilson always takes this path.' My witness thinks it's kinda odd Dobein should whisper somethin' like that, but he keeps walkin'. Then he reads about the murder in the papers."

"He must have heard the two shots," growled the inspector. "Why didn't he speak up right away?"

"My witness is deaf, but he reads lips good," replied Nick quickly. "He can testify to what Dobein told the other man, the gunman, I figure, and the jury will — "

Nick the Nose finished the sentence out in the hall, where the inspector threw him.

Why?

Nick's alleged witness was deaf and couldn't hear two shots, yet he remembered what Dobein said to the gunman because he "whispered."

The Case of
WILLIE THE WISP

Dr. Haledjian was vacationing in Europe when Count Schwinn, head of the customs in the country, requested help on a "perplexing problem of suspected smuggling."

Schwinn had scarcely entered Haledjian's hotel suite when he blurted, "Are you acquainted with Eugene W. McNally?"

"Better known as Willie the Wisp?" asked Haledjian. "He fenced diamonds in America for years and never got caught."

"That's the man," replied Schwinn. "He's got a new game. Six months ago he showed up at our customs post at Durien driving a new black convertible Fiorta, a foreign car that costs eleven thousand dollars. Naturally, we checked every inch of it. Nothing. But each of his three pieces of luggage had a false bottom."

Schwinn shook his head in exasperation. "In the

false bottoms were three jars — one filled with molasses, one with ground oyster shells, and one with bits of colored glass. We couldn't hold him for hiding such things, naturally. Now twice a month here comes a big black expensive Fiorta into the country at Durien. Willie again! Hidden in his bags are the jars filled with the same curious contents, molasses, glass, and shells.

"The brazen crook just sits and smirks at my customs men. They're forced to admit him into the country!" concluded Schwinn.

"Molasses, shells, and colored glass," mused Haledjian.

"What do they add up to?" cried Schwinn. "What's he smuggling?"

Haledjian lit a pipe and drew upon it reflectively. At length he grinned. "Deuced clever fellow, Willie."

What was Willie smuggling?

Willie the Wisp, a man with a shady reputation, knew he couldn't pass customs regularly without soon arousing suspicion, and he therefore created some. The jars and their contents, which baffled deduction, made sense to Haledjian only as decoys. Hence Willie was smuggling black convertible Fiorta automobiles!

The Case of the
WOODEN
BRIDGE

Archie Tate, mayor of Hays, collapsed in the reviewing stand at the Veterans Day parade just as the army drill team marched past.

"Tate died of a bullet wound inflicted by a high-powered rifle within the hour," Sheriff Monahan told Dr. Haledjian the next day.

"Who hated Tate enough to kill him?" said Haledjian.

"Orv Prill, maybe — I took his statement." The sheriff lifted a sheet from his desk and read Prill's words:

"I was resting under the trees near the old wooden bridge when the army drill team passed over it. They were a sight to see, stepping in perfect unison, rifles shining, and buttons glistening in the overhead sun."

"Prill," said the sheriff, "claims he lay near the bridge and didn't walk the half mile into town till

159

night. There wasn't anybody out there to verify his story. But nobody saw him in town, either."

"Why did the drill team cross the bridge on foot?"

"It's too rickety for those heavy army vehicles, so Lieutenant Cord had his men walk across," said the sheriff. "They joined the parade behind the high school band around noon."

"You think Prill knew beforehand the route the drill team was to take into town and made up an alibi about being there all afternoon?" asked Haledjian.

The sheriff nodded. "I believe he lied about seeing the soldiers cross the bridge. By then he had to be holed in town ready to shoot Tate.

"But," concluded the sheriff. "His story about the bridge is so simple it can't be disproved."

Haledjian disagreed. Do you?

No body of soldiers ever steps "in perfect unison" across a rickety old wooden bridge (as Prill claimed) for fear of setting up vibrations that might collapse the structure. Lieutenant Cord would have ordered in a route step at the bridge.